JEZEREAL

A Woman's Life
Memoirs

C. JENKINS

LAGRANGE GEORGIA

JEZEREAL

Copyright © 2024 by C. JENKINS

Printed in the United States of America. No part of this publication may be used or reproduced, stored in a retrieval system, transmitted in any form or by any means-electronic, mechanical, photocopy, recording, or any other except for brief quotations in printed reviews, without the publisher's prior written permission.

iSeebookz Publishing
Suite 137B Commerce Ave #300
Lagrange GA 30241

Editor & Cover Design: Y.D. Rowland

ISBN 979-8-9854863-9-1

First Edition
10 9 8 7 6 5 4 3 2 1

Printed in the United States

This is a work of fiction. Some historical accounts have been embellished. To preserve the authenticity of the author's voice and the essence of thoughts, minimal editing has been performed in segments. We extend our appreciation for your support.

C.JENKINS /iSeebookz Publishing

CONTENTS

Dedication Given To

My Mom & My "Irish Twin", Sister, Karen

I dedicate this book to my mother and to my "little" sister, as they were/are truly the two who aspired me to pursue my lifelong inspiration to follow my dreams... strive for the light, and fight against the darkness of my days and nights and yet revive myself to rise again and ascend to the next step on the spiral of life.

PROLOGUE:

Present Day Thoughts

It had been a hard cold night of snow. Everything was frozen. Many things needed to be attended to, but they wouldn't be for a woman alone on a farm. Those who generally assisted wouldn't be able to get there that day. The snow was too high on the passes. However, the weather, be as it may, she still rose. It was her habit. Rise early to see what is on the horizon...to contemplate and plan what must be, could be, and couldn't be done. But on this day, she was just too tired. She rose, yes, then looked out the window, shook her head "No," and crawled back into bed.

Her life was changing once again, and she wasn't pleased about it. She had decisions to make in several areas of her life. Her eyes needed spectacles because when she shot her rifle, she was off the mark. Different things were off in her body, so she was exploring different herbs.

Friends and family were either dying, dead, or tired and didn't write anymore. She was trying to figure out how to live the rest of her life alone. She had so striven to help others- not to live the life she had, not afraid, but learning how to fight against the night. Although, with life, she knew she had failed at times.

She had lived through so many things...born into slavery, she had to watch the murder of her momma, herself raped and thrown by the road, only to be found by peace-giving people;

she had to learn to live in peace with the world. When she opened herself to the Christian doctrines and tried to understand and accept them, the world went haywire again.

She struggled with the practices of the world, spiritual, political, and with everyday people. She'd grown up in an unjust world but had been taught that God would bring justice if she simply believed in Him. She'd tried to do right all of her life, but many times she had to take a step back and ask herself if she was wrong and maybe went too far in seeking justice.

Even though she wasn't born into it, the now 58-year-old woman, reminiscing, did what she thought she could -to make it back to Eden.

One

JEZEREAL ON THE WAY TO MARYLAND

A horizontal plume of white warm steam issued profusely from beneath the goliath black engine of the Philadelphia, Wilmington, and Baltimore, also known as the P.W. & B. passenger train. Clearly not suspecting the hot cloud that engulfed her, Jezereal Wright startled, sprang out just beyond the benign expression of steam. "Whew, Jesus!" She fanned frantically behind her coat only to find the steam settling. Collecting herself, she checked her body, smoothed the back of her coat, then feeling a bit embarrassed, she scanned the platform, hopeful of an immediate rendezvous with her brother; well, really, her lifelong friend, Gil.

They were to be on their way together to Maryland, and she was not used to traveling alone. He was not forthcoming. While a little disappointed, it wasn't unexpected. She'd have to wait for him as was usual. She took tentative steps toward the station house, but seeing men spilling about its door, she hesitated. She found a lonely pillar of wood off to the right of the station, just toward the end of the building, placed her bag on the floor, leaned back against the pillar, and waited.

As she waited, she reviewed the train that would carry them to the next stage of her life. She could see the conductor walking the aisle of the passenger seating compartment, checking seats, and preparing the coach for incoming passengers. She could hear the engineer and the coal man discussing issues regarding the upcoming trip, which she equally couldn't quite hear as the men at the station were loudly debating another issue that she couldn't discern.

She'd traveled by train once previously with her mother. But it had been a short trip from this very station at her home to the neighboring city just to showcase the grand opening of the line. It had been festive and fun, a thing to do. Her mother, Kaylean Wright, had welcomed the advent of the train, while others at the time had condemned train travel as a blight on society. Many had mused that it would never take the place of the carriage. Surely, it had its troubles, but the opening day had been every bit of grand. Jezereal had dreamed from that day a time when she and others would ride the train as a matter of course and convenience. She reminisced about that and wondered what Kaylean would think about her child paying for the trip that would take her all the way to Baltimore.

The afternoon air was crisp and breezy. Fingers of cold wind searched and found an opening at the nape of her neck. She bunched the black woolen fabric of her cape closer to her neck. It was tied tightly, but somehow, the cold still found its way in. Shortly the wind changed, which brought her a strong, lonely scent of lilac. She breathed deeply to assure herself of its identity.

Unmistakable, the brief smell of March was quick to bloom and die away, so one should inhale deeply for as long as possible, for it wouldn't be until the following year when it could be breathed again. *Where could the aroma of lilacs come from at the edge of a train station?* She thought. Pursuing the scent that led her up to the train station landing, she squinted to partially block out the afternoon sunlight, partially to sharpen her sight.

She scanned the area immediately to the side of the station for a minute before stepping down behind it. She had time and was a bit nervous about standing there waiting anyway. Plus, she wasn't all that sure now that she was at the train station that she wanted to go anywhere. So, she turned away from the steps to drop off the sidewalk. There she found it, a lone lilac bush in the patch of otherwise grey-black bushes six feet from where she stood. It was spring, and while other bushes still lay dormant, the lilac had already rushed headlong into the season.

She went to the lilac bush, gently fanning the branches, she breathed its aroma deeply. She looked toward the sky, finding the sun so bright she had to squeeze her eyes shut. She reopened them again to see. It was a clear, new day, full of remembrance of the life she was leaving, and the potential of the future; promises from no one, only a promise to herself.

Standing there, reminiscing and wondering, she was drawn back to the station or, more immediately, to sounds in the station that had no place there and that she could discern and make sense of across the station platform in an equally out-of-the-way spot as her own. She focused her attention on a high-pitched sound of despair and found a man with his arm raised, which he quickly brought down on the face of a woman.

He slapped her hard, so hard that she stumbled backward. He raised his hand to hit her again. The woman held an infant of a little more than a year. Before he could hit her again, Jezereal had made short of the distance between where she had stood and where their drama was unfolding. She landed just steps between them, seemingly flailing, awkwardly knocking the man's hand back. She grabbed the woman and baby as the three of them stumbled backward. Jezereal planted a foot and righted them. Both strangers were shocked and perplexed by her arrival in their midst. As Jezereal righted the woman, the woman took a step back out of fear, looking from Jezereal quickly to her assailant to see if he was still coming at her. When he didn't move, she returned her attention to Jezereal. They had been so caught up in their own drama. Both eyed her in fear, tinged with amazement.

She stood and shook herself. She tossed back her head and smoothed her hair and clothing as if dusting herself off. "My goodness! Clumsy, clumsy, me. Forgive me! Oh, I'm just mortified. I tripped, you see," and prattled on as if she had not witnessed the initial violence.

Once straightened out, she turned to croon over how beautiful the baby was, completely ignoring their look of confusion as they began to try to grasp the situation. The man's initial aim had been lost, and in his struggle to grasp the situation, he vacillated between berating her for being clumsy and stupid and feeling very much in the public's view as men from the station had turned their attention to them. He had no way of knowing that they had witnessed Jezereal running across the station platform in front of them, only to act as if she were falling to the ground.

Even the men were wondering amongst themselves what she was up to. The woman was just confused, the entire situation being too much to figure out as she attempted to come to her senses from the slap. The baby howled, readily expressing its disapproval of the entire situation.

Jez slowed her talk and lowered her voice. "Oh, I'm sorry, I've startled the baby. She slowly approached the woman. "You poor child, you. It's OK now. It's ok. I'm not going to hurt you. It's okay." She spoke the words to the baby, all the while holding the momma's eyes with her own. The mother's eyes, which had been wide, began to relax through Jezereal's soothing words.

"It's ok, Little Mother, isn't it?" The mother began to soothe the baby, "It's ok, Johnnie, it's ok. Shh, shh." The baby, not so sure it was okay, continued to howl. Jezereal stepped closer, "Oh, please, may I try?" She extended her arms. The woman hesitantly but hopefully handed her baby over.

Jezereal took the baby into her arms and gently rocked and cradled him to her breast. "Ah, now, it's ok." She walked and rocked, and the baby's screams subsided to a whimper and then to quiet. As she continued to walk back and forth between them, she kissed the baby's cheeks. When she got to the man, Jez congratulated him on having a fine, healthy baby boy. The thoughts against the intrusion that ran through the man's mind quieted, and the fact that he didn't unleash them upon the woman relieved the wife.

While baby talking to the infant, Jezereal observed the wife's face and demeanor; she readily understood that this wasn't the first time the woman had taken a hit from her husband, by hand or word. Evidence from the bluish, purple tint surrounding her left eye showed that one of the two had been recent. She praised, melodramatically, the man for producing such a beautiful child.

His irritation at her disturbance abated further in the profuse praise of his manhood, and he took on a jovial demeanor. Holding the baby close one last time and kissing his cheek gently, Jezereal passed the baby back to his mother. Making conversation, Jezereal asked the mother where they were going. The mother told her they were going to visit her sister in Maryland.

Gil had approached from behind the man. He was on the ground, but he'd gauged that he could clear the platform and take the man down by the back of his legs. Gil saw Jezereal clear the platform in that direction. While he had no idea what the situation was about, he knew she was propelling herself into a fight. He'd shaken his head and headed in. Before he reached them, Jezereal had noticed him just as she'd asked to hold the baby.

She sent Gil a message with her eyes, which stopped him short of his launch to the platform. He was not quite sure what it meant beyond that and raised an eyebrow, but then he heard her cooing, speaking to the baby of his robust and powerful father, and while clearly a lie, Gil had backed into the station's shadows, listening and waiting. Just as the man began to inquire as to where such a lovely young woman was going on her own, Gil hopped up behind them, his boots thumping on the platform, making both wife and husband jump a second time that evening, and said,

"I should have known my little sister would find the most handsome fellow at the station to flirt with, and he ruffles the hair of the infant boy. The man was taken aback, at first thinking Gil was praising him, but then he tried to hide his embarrassment as he realized Gil was speaking of the child.

Gil had stood to the side of the station office. From the beginning, he had watched the whole scene in which Jezereal, a bystander, had become an intricate player. Gil had meant to make her wait longingly and then to surprise her. He hadn't seen her in over three years, and he had no desire to be anything other than what she'd always known: a loose fellow, at odds with life, in need of the strong hand of a good woman.

So, when he saw her, he merely thought to make her wait. She wouldn't worry or suppose that anything happened to him, nothing other than what she'd known to happen before. It wasn't long before he witnessed that she was still none other than her old self championing the cause of the seemingly helpless. He'd witnessed the altercation between the couple and felt his blood surge; his pulse quickened when the man with an opened hand had brought it down on the woman's face. He had been on the move to stop anything further, but Jezereal had been quicker than he had to react.

Damn, she could always see trouble rising before he did, so he stopped himself in his tracks, breathed deeply, exhaled, folded his arms across his chest, and settled back against the wall of the station house to see what would transpire. He saw her move quickly and deftly, a form, a style he well remembered.

She'd blocked the man's hand in midair with the cloaked arm of her left as it threatened to land, and with her right foot, she'd swept the woman off balance. Just as swiftly, she'd caught the woman with her right arm and backed her and the baby back to standing. It happened so fast that neither the man nor the woman was sure of her intervention. She righted the woman, saying, "Oh, my goodness, you looked off balance! I thought for sure you and the baby would take a tumble."

Both the man and woman were speechless amidst the howls of the baby. The man stammered something mixed with shock and anger, then realizing the situation, which took a minute, he offered a feeble thanks. Gil just shook his head at that in admiration. There was light, albeit uneasy, talk between the three of them for a few minutes. Actually, the woman said nothing besides words of comfort to the baby and equally feeble words of thanks.

It appeared that she didn't know quite how the situation would unfold and thus couldn't be sure enough to relax and thank the strange woman. She kept looking at the man warily with fear but also with worry about the next few minutes. When his demeanor changed to one of civility with the strange woman and as the baby began to calm, she relaxed a bit.

The train whistled, signaling time to board, so enough watching for Gil. He jumped onto the platform, and as he approached the column, he could see the look "It's over" in Jezereal's eyes. She started praising the guy who, from all signs, was unsophisticated yet working hard to appear to be so. He slowed his approach toward the gathering to hear Jezereal say, "Oh, my goodness, what a beautiful little boy! But how could you be anything but handsome? He's your son? Yes?" The man beamed and said, "That he is. You can see the resemblance, can't you? Others want to say that he looks like his momma, but if you see the strong chin of a man, then you're definitely seeing me!"

Gil escorted Jez onto the train, all the while smirking and smiling, each admiring the changes in the other. It had been so long since they'd seen each other. Not much was said than commenting on where their seats were located and how to best navigate getting there. The train was packed, and there was much hustle and bustle in getting to their seats. They had to wait passively while others moved into their perspective places.

After locating their seats, Gil and Jez arranged their light luggage in their seating area while others waited passively for them to do so. Once comfortably seated, Gil looked at Jez. She knew something along the lines of what he was about to say, "You still strap on those white wings when you feel like it, but I know you're still a she-devil." "Gil, don't even start with me. I was just trying to help a fellow human being out. I didn't hurt anybody. Let's let it go and have a nice trip together."

They both rolled their eyes, shook their heads at each other, smiled, and relaxed in their seats. The train began to move forward toward its destination. After about 15 minutes and the buzz of conversation amongst passengers began to calm, Gil turned to Jez, "You know, you're looking kinda grown up now. Almost didn't recognize you until I saw the moves. How ya been?

How is Miss K? I heard she was sick, and you left her, so she must not be all that sick." Jezereal winced. "She's really sick, Gil, but she wouldn't let me stay." Jezereal held her breath briefly, trying to hold back her tears. "She made me go."

She had to stop and look away from him. But he knew if she "made her go," it wasn't going to be anything good for either of them. He decided to change the subject. With Jez, on some things, particularly of the heart, you had to let her leak information. Full confrontation, would be received with intent to retaliate. Don't touch a wild animal's wound; you're likely to get bitten.

"So, after all these years, I still gotta have you following me around." Jez turned to him, feigning indignation. "Follow you! You're following me! Who contacted who, Sir? And I use the 'Sir' loosely." "Look, little Girl, no need to be rude. I was just playing with you as we always have." He hesitated and looked out the window at the land rushing past. "It's been a long time since we played together; I've been to many places and done many things. Some I'm proud of, some I'm not, but in all of it, I must say, I've missed us. I was 19; you were what 15?" "Yes, it's been two years."

She wanted to tell him how mad she'd been at him, hurt, and lonely when he left, but she didn't say it to him then. He'd gone out to California to seek "his fortune." They were quiet for a while, each considering their lives between the last time they had seen each other. "Gil, it's been too much. I'm tired."

Gil didn't even look at her. He kept his eyes on the window and the passing landscape. He put out his hand toward hers. She looked at it and placed her hand in his. She would accompany him to Maryland.

As for the train, the world quieted down to the steady beat of travels on the tracks. Jez fell asleep. As she slept, she dreamt of Kaylean and when, as a child, Kaylean, who had always told her, "Our God is a prayer-hearing God," was maybe or about to be gone.

~ Two ~

YOUNG JEZEREAL

Now close it and recite, please. Jezereal Wright, seven years old, smoothed the pages of her Bible, closed the book gently, and then her eyes. She waited until the words began to form themselves one after another in her mind, then she began...

> *Hosea 1*
>
> *1:1 The word of the LORD that came unto Hosea, the son of Beeri, in the days of Uzziah, Jotham, Ahaz, and Hezekiah, kings of Judah, and in the days of Jeroboam the son of Joash, king of Israel.*
>
> *1:2 The beginning of the word of the LORD by Hosea. And the Lord said to Hosea, Go take unto thee a wife of whoredoms and children of whoredoms: for the land hath committed great whoredom, departing from the Lord.*
>
> *1:3 So he went and took Gomer the daughter of Diblaim; which conceived, and bare him a son.*
>
> *1:4 And the LORD said unto him, Call his name Jezreel; for yet a little while, and I will avenge the blood of Jezreel upon the*

house of Jehu, and will cause to cease the kingdom of the house of Israel.

1:5 And it shall come to pass on that day, that I will break the bow of Israel, in the valley of Jezreel.

1:6 And she conceived again, and bare a daughter. And God said unto him, call her name Loruhamah: for I will no more have mercy upon the house of Israel; but I will utterly take them away.

1:7 But I will have mercy upon the house of Judah, and will save them by the LORD their God, and will not save them by bow, nor by sword, nor by battle, by horses, nor by horsemen.

1:8 Now when she had weaned Loruhamah, she conceived, and bare a son.

1:9 Then said God, Call his name Loammi: for ye are not my people, and I will not be your God.

1:10 Yet the number of the children of Israel shall be as the sand of the sea, which cannot be measured nor numbered; and it shall come to pass, that in the place where it was said unto them, Ye are not my people, there it shall be said unto them, Ye are the sons of the living God.

1:11 Then shall the children of Judah and the children of Israel be gathered together, and appoint themselves one head, and they shall come up out of the land: for great shall be the day of Jezreel.

She repeated part of the last line: for great shall be the day of Jezreel. She opened her eyes and examined her mother's face with unspoken consternation. Had she gotten it all right? She needn't have worried. Kaylean Wright sat leaning heavily back into her chair, her eyes closed as if savoring the words. She opened her eyes slowly, "Yes, yes, that's it. For great shall be the day of Jezreel." They both smiled.

"Now go on outside and play child." Jezereal couldn't think about playing, which always required some thought, as she was in a place called Jezreel Valley, beautiful, lush, and much coveted by kings, a beautiful place. She walked in the Valley of her namesake.

Between sleep and wakefulness, her thoughts came to the present day before returning to a deeper slumber. Jezereal often remembered the day she had mastered that particular passage. Even now, with the entire Bible committed to memory, she marveled at herself and at her memory for the written word. Anytime she had decided to remember what she'd read, she could do it. Kaylean revered the written word and wanted her daughter-adopted daughter, to love it as much as she did. Memorizing was her way to place the value of words in Jezereal's heart. At the time, she had no idea that her gift to Jezereal would save a nation.

The train's rhythm over the tracks took her back to deep slumber as her mind continued to reminisce. Playing was not a thing Jezereal did well. As a matter of fact, she had never really had the occasion to play before she came to live with the Wrights. In the time allotted for play, she generally sat upon a tree stump in the middle of her backyard, and she looked out upon the woods behind her house and dreamed. At seven, she spent a lot of time in her dreams.

During the day, her heart and mind attempted to repair the feelings and terrors of her dreams at night. On numerous occasions, Kaylean had attempted to take her to play with other children and to church picnics, where other children invited her to play, but she continued almost mute behaviors when surrounded by other children. Sometimes, she would strike a pose and just stare. Occasionally, if a child touched her, whatever the child would say, she would echo it back. The children loved playing that little game with her. The last time it occurred, Kaylean had to stop the children. It became a strange, weird scene...the children one after another touching her daughter and her daughter mimicking their ways. The voices her daughter was able to mimic were frightening. One little girl dragged her older sister into the game, and Jez mimicked the older girl's voice exactly. Everyone got a little scared after that and merely stared at the child for a while...her eyes were wide, her body posed as if she were pouring tea, and this much older voice emanating from her.

Kaylean picked her daughter up and carried her to the carriage. It wasn't until she and Joshua were on the way home in the carriage that Jezereal seemed to come out of her state. She roused and told Joshua a dog was in the road up ahead. Neither had seen or heard a dog, but sure enough, as they rounded the bend, a dog began to howl and bark viciously alongside the carriage as they drove.

After that experience, Kaylean stopped pushing. She realized the child was full of extreme anxiety and could only wonder what had happened to make a child go into such an odd state when she was around other children. She wondered if she should risk inquiring further about the child around the area in which she and Joshua had found her raped and beaten on the roadside. She realized, though, that whatever happened to her had been really bad, and there was no sense in digging any of that up again. No child had been reported missing. They had checked the area for months, but there had been no call or cry for a missing child among white or black folks in the area. So, they decided to keep her as their own.

About six months after her arrival at the Wrights, she ventured, for the first time, into her front yard alone. She sneaked a peek around the side of the house. Her yard and those adjourning were empty. Nothing moved. She slid around the house with her back to the wall. Once in the front, still against the wall, she squatted, making herself small. She surveyed the street, hoping that no one would see her. When she was sure she was alone, she slowly rose, hesitated, and then stepped forward into the yard. She was Jezereal and claimed her ground as the Valley of Jezreel.

Just when she was accepting her space, a boy strolled around the corner of a house down the street. She didn't see him as she had closed her eyes and was seeing herself standing on a hill surveying the valley below. "Hey, Girl!" His words chilled her, and without opening her eyes, she reeled on her heels and fled. "Stop!" Her every instinct kept her running until he yelled again, "Little Girl! Wait, I wanna talk to you!" She stopped so hard it was as if her body had slammed into a brick wall, although every nerve in her body raced away. Although she couldn't move, her body was wracked with tremors. He ran across the yards and slapped his hand down on her right shoulder.

At the touch of his hand, Jezereal stopped shaking. It was immediate, and it was profound. He tugged at her shoulder to turn her towards him, and she complied. He was laughing. "Girl, why'd you run?" As she faced him, he, for the first time in his eleven years, felt fear, well, at least a kind he didn't know. As he had no experience with that kind of fear, he couldn't quite comprehend or even describe what he saw in the little girl's eyes. But it was enough of something to make him jerk his hand away from her and step back. It was in her eyes, the thing that frightened him, that instinctually told him to back away. As frightening as it was, there was also something else that he nor- mally should have seen first, beauty. She had the most beautiful eyes that he'd ever seen. Grey eyes, maybe even silver, but there was a hardness in those eyes. He saw in her a look as if she were an animal in the first movements of prowling, inching closer to him. She hadn't even moved, but it was in her eyes. There was no fear in her eyes.

He had merely wanted to play, to make friends with the little girl who was new to the area. Neither one said a word as he backed away from her. He'd actually wanted to run, but he knew better than that. You don't turn your back when you walk up on a wild animal. You keep your eyes on it and back away, slow. And, then, realizing that a little girl had made him feel fear, he stopped. He wanted to know the nature of his fear, so unusual it was so unexpected. He didn't know what to say in the face of this creature. He thought she was beautiful. There was lightning in her eyes, which made her frightening at the same time. His voice caught in his throat the first time he tried to speak. He cleared his throat and apologized. "I'm sorry if I scared you. I didn't mean to. I just wanted to say hello."

For Jezereal, the boy's words were like the sound of a train's horn that you hear in the distance, and it grows as it comes nearer. Then it's so loud that you can almost barely stand it when it's passing in front of you. She could see him speaking, but she wasn't sure what he was saying to her, and then, as if a door were opening or a curtain rising, the sound from the world came back to her. She was looking at him, and then she could hear a bird chirping nearby and the wind rustling through the trees. She struggled to make sense of the words coming out of the boy's mouth. "I didn't...say hello." She bent her neck, and it crackled inside her head. She waited because it was all so very strange. The boy waited too, and then he said, half nervously laughing, "Did I scare you?" She heard his words as if they were banging off the walls inside of a church. All she could say was, "scare me?" He said again, "I didn't mean to scare you. I was just trying to say hello."

Jezereal examined the boy who stood in front of her. He was bigger than her, almost a foot taller, and he had orange-colored hair, but his face was kind of red against white skin. She still didn't have any words. The look in her eye was fading, and as it faded, his confidence grew. He relaxed. "Where did you move from?" Jezereal didn't respond. She continued to study him as she began to understand what he was saying. "Anyway, my name is Robert, although my friends call me Gil. You can call me Gil if you want. Robert Andrew Gilford, that's my name."

Jezereal had never had any boy speak to her in a way that she could later trust would be good, so she made no effort to reply. She backed away from him. She backed to the edge of the house and back down the side of the house toward her backyard. She, too, had learned not to turn her back on a known thing, let alone an unknown one. Later in life, she might learn to have no fear, but that would be then. She didn't want to wait for him to keep speaking and say something or ask something hurtful, so she simply wanted to be away from him.

Robert eyed her quizzically. "Strange girl" was all he could think as he watched her disappear around the back of her house. When she was gone, he stood for a second and stared at her house, not really seeing it. His mind whirled. "I wonder if I should follow her. No, you've already scared her enough. You don't want her to start screaming or something equally silly. She's a little girl. Leave her alone. She's a strange one." He turned and headed back home. He didn't dare admit to himself that he wasn't sure if he could handle seeing her eyes again that day.

Kaylean had seen that look once herself. It had been on that carriage ride home that day with the children at the church picnic, and the dog had been incessantly barking at them for a long way down the road as they made their way home. Joshua tried to be nice at first, "Hello, little fellow, what might your name be? What do you all think the little fellow's name is?" Kaylean offered, "Dog?" Joshua laughed. Joshua turned to Jezereal and asked, "My Jezzie, what do you think the little one's name is?"

Jezereal did not answer. He repeated his question. Her eyes were on the dog. This made Joshua uncomfortable. So, he began yelling at the dog, "Go home, you little rascal. Leave us be!" Jezereal had come to herself and found a mad dog running at the family, and she began intensely examining the dog. Kaylean had been holding her when Jezereal stood up. As she stood, her foot caught on the hem of Kaylean's dress, and before anyone could do anything, Jez had toppled out of the carriage onto the road.

Joshua pulled hard on the reins to turn the carriage out of the path where Jezereal was falling back by the rear wheels and halted the horses as soon as he could. Kaylean was screaming because the dog had veered away from them and was leaping toward Jezereal. Jez rolled over and over upon the ground and, in one swift final roll, came to rest upon her hands and knees. The dog charged upon her. Kaylean screamed as Joshua leaped from the carriage, whip in hand. Jezereal didn't move as the dog charged upon her. She merely stared at the dog. Her eyes were intense and steady. The baby never wavered in body or eyes.

Kaylean had never seen that look in man nor child, anything living for that matter. And, evidently, the dog hadn't either. In his charge, he locked eyes with the child, and something in him gave way and he lost his nerve, but he couldn't stop his forward thrust. He tried to stop but ended up tripping and tumbled himself. Jezereal moved slightly, and he fell alongside her whimpering. Joshua got to Jez just as the dog raised his head, and he whisked her up into his arms and away from the dog.

He ran back and leaped up into the carriage with Jez. Kaylean grabbed her, hugged and kissed her head. She was quiet. Joshua and Kaylean were quiet save for a look between them. Joshua only raised an eyebrow and shook his head. The look was the closest notion he could give, a man not given to cursing to say, "That's the damndest thing I've ever seen." But Jezereal was prone to show him many things he'd never seen before. Later, a few miles from home, Jezereal began to shake, and Kaylean could only hold her tight and soothe her with words of comfort and love.

"You're ok, little sweetie. I'm here, and Joshua is here. We're not going to let anything bad happen to you ever again. It's OK now. That old dog. He was just so gruff and mean acting. He wasn't going to really hurt you now, was he? See you're ok. You're ok baby. We're going to get home, and I'm going to put you in your bedclothes, and you're going to get some rest. I'm sorry baby. It's been such a long day. Just let me hold you. Rest now, huh. We'll be home soon, and everything will be ok." When they arrived home, Jez was sound asleep. Joshua carried her into the house. Kaylean undressed her and put Jez into her bedclothes. Joshua pulled the blankets over her, and then Joshua and Kaylean whispered long into the evening about the events of the day and this strange child God had given them.

Kaylean and her husband, Pastor Joshua Wright, were missionaries. But God was almost impossible for Jez to grasp in her earlier years. God was more like an interesting theory to Jezereal. He was someone who didn't come through and had never worked for her the way people said he would. However, she loved reading the Bible because it was the best book explaining people's behaviors that she could have. She experimented with religion, trying to do the things that others did in an effort to maybe feel what they felt. And, the meditations that the God-loving folk wrote were useful and gave her a calming effect; she had the hope to believe.

But for Jez, she actually believed that you have to give back what you get, and that's what humans understood. She was a high proponent of helping those who were used and abused by others and couldn't stomach mistreatment for the sake of meanness or control. As a woman, a former slave, she saw men with power and control as her definition of evil. And, as the South upheld slavery, the institution and those who lived by it, in Jez's estimation, were evil in nature.

Kaylean was inordinately busy around the house, as busy as she could be with the consumption weighing against her. Even ill, Kaylean would push through pain, exhaustion, and fits of coughing blood. She couldn't allow herself the luxury to be weakened, not today. She was anxious, and her soul was full. Kaylean periodically felt herself giving into tears, but she'd push them back because she believed Jezzie would be hurt and confused if she saw her crying. She had taught her that big girls in the real world didn't cry over the inevitable things in life and that all children are expected to grow up and move forward with their lives. They left at different ages, and that's inevitable.

She had left her family home at an age even younger than Jez. So, this was an occasion to be marked with happiness shown through smiles, lots of sweet words, and gentle physical affections. She would send Jezereal away from her before she died. Jezereal had already seen too much for any one being, let alone a child with already so much pain to bear, to add having to watch her waste away. This was best in Kaylean's eyes; she loved that girl too much.

This was best in Kaylean's eyes. She knew Jez would be angry with her for not allowing her to be there for her final moments. Still, Kaylean wanted her to remember her as strong and defiant, not wasted and helpless. Kaylean had difficulty smiling as Jezzie would be left alone, and her inner wisdom gave insight that Jezereal being alone could be dangerous business. This was not an age, in Kaylean's mind, for her only daughter to be left without a mother on a potentially friendless path. She would have to send Jezereal to Baltimore for her sister to watch over her. Kaylean wrote a lengthy note to Robert Gilford and asked him to come. Discerning that she only had a short time left-she'd do what she could to ensure Jezereal had others to look after her. There was enough money available to support her and guarantee her well-being. Still, she'd have to work at something to sustain her emotionally, if not financially.

Joshua had always withheld his most intense emotions from Jez; he thought that best. Intense emotions to him, either way, were anathema to living a peaceful life. Strong emotions give way in the end to sorrow and discontent. Steady, even-keeled, put one foot in front of the other, and "Stay the course" was Joshua's motto. Even Joshua Wright, the man who welcomed her into his life as her father, who Jezzie learned to love as a father, never really knew who she was. But Jez learned, living with him, that she had to be noticeable, or at least her skills had to be. He never questioned the percentage of black blood flowing within her.

But, the mother who took her in, whom she learned to love as a mother, understood her most and had some inkling of her heritage. Kaylean protected that part of Jezzie's life. Who needed to know, and for what purpose? She could see somewhat into Jez's dark spaces, but she wasn't well enough to know how to help Jezereal. But at least she understood some of her pain. And, for all of her life, that's all Jezereal could ever have asked of either of her mothers.

Kaylean had been of a different character than Joshua. She, when happy, could be loud, particularly in terms of her intense laughter from her gut. If something hit Kaylean as funny, her laughter could raise the roof. Initially, laughter was disconcerting to Jezereal. She'd heard so little of it in a good way. It didn't quite frighten her; she was more wary than afraid. What would come next? Would it be a laugh at her expense, one that would reveal a mistake she'd made? Was something about to happen in which she would emerge from it with a bruise, perhaps doubled over or in some equally painful existence?

Initially, in her experiences with laughter, those laughing would look at her with a look of expectation that she should be laughing too, but she rarely got the joke. Now, that was frightening. So, she learned to make the sounds and facial expressions of laughter before understanding why something was funny to those around her.

She didn't know what it was to feel that thing that made something funny. It took her a while to learn and distinguish what "funny" was. But, when it happened...a little bit of her heart, along with her mind and a significant portion of her spirit, rejoiced. She learned to laugh with the Wrights.

For instance, one winter, the snow had descended unmercifully for almost a day. There would be little movement anywhere beyond the house, but the chickens and the pigs had to be attended to. So, Kaylean decided later than usual, about 8 a.m., it was time to go out and check on them. Usually, Joshua would have attended to their needs before he began his visits for the day or started working on his sermons for Sunday.

However, he'd been ill, wheezing, coughing, and hot with fever for more than a day. Kaylean admonished him to stay in bed, and when he tried to get up, she'd told him in no uncertain terms, "Joshua Wright, you will lie right where you are. Don't move any part of you- to get up and go toward that door. You can't do much for your family or your flock in the cemetery!" Joshua started to protest but was wracked with a cough. Kaylean smirked, "Yes, now, see that? You sound as if you're ready to toss me your lungs right now. Jezereal, come here beside me."

Jezereal did as was commanded. "Get ready. Come on now, you know how to catch it." Kaylean had crouched down in front of Joshua expectantly, and Jezereal followed suit. Joshua was still coughing. "Now, when the lung comes out, don't drop it!" Jezereal looked at Kaylean, who feigned seriousness, and then back at Joshua. A giggle erupted, and when they saw her laugh, Kaylean dropped her pose and began laughing as well. Even in a fit of a cough, Joshua began laughing and coughed all the harder. Learning to laugh and to watch someone being fondly teased opened the way for Jezereal to relax and not fear other children.

Kaylean had encouraged Jezereal's play with Robert Gilford, as Jezereal had never found friendship with children her age. Jez started following Robert when he walked down the street in front of the house. Robert talked to Jezereal, but Jezereal remained silent as always. Kaylean didn't call her back into the house. The first time it happened, her heart skipped a beat. Jezereal was standing in the spot just off the side of the corner of the house like she'd done for weeks. She never moved far from that spot. She'd just stand there and stare out into the yard. For weeks, Kaylean stealthily spied on Jezereal after she told her to go out and play.

At first, Jez only stayed in the backyard, but one day, after their daily Bible readings, Jezereal left her stump and ventured into the front yard. Kaylean didn't know what happened between when Jez had gone out the back door and when she came in because Kaylean had knocked over a bowl of mashed potatoes scheduled for dinner while trying to get from the kitchen to the front door. Kaylean had tried to clean it up quickly. But when Jezereal came back in the door, the child looked like she had seen God. There was no color in her complexion, and she walked to her seat in front of the fireplace and sat. Ten minutes later, Jez started shaking violently. Kaylean had learned this response.

Jezereal had met with something outside that was out of the ordinary for her. But it was different when she went to comfort Jezereal, as they had worked out a comforting ritual. Jezereal had shaken for only a few minutes before her body relaxed. Kaylean had expected her to drift off into sleep as was normal, but Jezereal, for the first time, reached out her little hand and stroked Kaylean's face. Kaylean's immediate impulse was to shout, "Hallelujah!" But, knowing her baby, she just smiled at her, and wonderfully, Jezereal smiled back. Something real, really good had happened out there.

It was only a matter of time before Jezereal started following a young red-haired boy down the road in front of their house to the end. She just followed, and at the end of the road, he'd turn and say a few words to her. She didn't respond, and he'd go on his way. Then, Jez would turn around and come back home. Once back in the house, it seemed to Kaylean that Jezereal would find a way to touch her, and she felt more at ease with touching Jezereal. Kaylean and Joshua, at night, after Jezereal went to sleep, would praise God.

Kaylean and Joshua knew, after the experiences at church gatherings, that they had to allow Jezereal to take others as she could. So, as much as she wanted to, Kaylean's heart screamed to figure out a way to somehow cultivate a relationship between Jezereal and the boy. Kaylean described a scheme to Joshua to learn more about this boy that Jez followed daily. However, Joshua countered her and settled her mind to merely watch and see what would happen with them. So, Kaylean stepped back, but that didn't mean she couldn't watch, and she did. Over the years, Kaylean watched the boy, whom she called Robert, even though Jezereal had named him Gil. Jezereal had taken some time to get used to calling people by their first name. It was work for Kaylean to help Jezereal journey from Ms. Kaylean to Kaylean to momma. Joshua had made the transition in Jezereal's mind later in her teen years to daddy, but before she did make it to Poppa Joshua. Gil had told her to call him "Gil" for Robert Gilford. It spoke to his given name... and as a child just a few years older than she, she didn't need any more of it to call him by. In any case, Gil taught Kaylean's daughter to ride a horse and handle a gun like a man.

While Kaylean could do all those things, she'd never shown her husband in any way or form that she was of that nature. So, Kaylean was happy that Jez learned those things. Kaylean had grown up, from what she confided one day to Jez, that she was the eldest of 7 children. Her mother had died after the birth of the last, and they were dirt poor. She'd struggled to help her father raise them, a good and Christian man as he could be given their financial lack. He worked hard but had no particular ability to do other than what he did. Work hard in the field all day to provide for them to have food and clothing. Kaylean learned early that her job was caring for the children and her father. She had no time to take care of herself, but one day, a missionary came along and left books with them, which included a Bible.

Joshua was a genteel easterner. He tended to be as precise as possible with his words and sermons. Which wasn't always the best thing because some of his congregational members sometimes had no clue what some of his words meant. He'd learned over time, however, to gauge his speech, primarily because he practiced at home. He'd learned to pay attention to Kaylean's reactions, like if she cringed, tapped her fingers on the table as if bored, or rolled her eyes, as if annoyed.

He became attuned to his congregations over the years and became very renowned for his sermons. But then, he was also so very courteous in speech and in behavior. He was very loving and caring with Kaylean. He never raised his voice to her, but every now and then, he would fold his hands together, bow his head, close his eyes as if going to pray, and simply say, "Kaylean, can you please shut up." That was the harshest he ever could be. He wouldn't ever preach about "fire and brimstone" because he remembered being terrified as a young child that anyone could burn in hell for an eternity. No, he would not engender fear as a way to make people try to run to heaven. He felt his ministry was to protect the weak and strove to be kind and generous in his dealings with people who may have felt of lesser status due to all the ways people chose to divide themselves.

At home, Kaylean worked to hone her daughter's memory and intelligence to solve problems and encouraged her natural propensity to move silently. She wittingly ignored her daughter's visits to the rough places that Gil took her. She intuited, learned her daughter's proclivities, and through just gutting it out and with profuse nights of prayer, and ultimately sheer hope that Jezereal could handle what she got into and that whatever that might be, Jez would be leveled-headed and able to figure a way out of trouble. Kaylean didn't want her daughter to be sheltered and stupid about life. She never realized that all of these things could be applied to a purpose that involved anything more than self-preservation. And, even so, now, she was afraid...more afraid than she'd ever been for anyone's life.

~ Three ~

JEZEREAL ON THE TRAIN

Jezereal awoke from her dream state and looked at her childhood friend, "Gil, I miss Momma so much! You know the only reason I'm on this train is because of momma. Why would I want to leave South Carolina and go to a cold state? But, I know my momma is dying, Gil. She won't tell me, admit it. She didn't allow the doctor to tell me anything, but I knew. I went along with it. When she would get into one of her episodes, I'd pretend with her that it wasn't such a great thing. Agreeing that she was getting stronger and that she just had a bad reaction to something she ate or that it was the weather that day. Like I said, I knew. What was I going to do? Momma is a good, righteous, strong woman, so I couldn't even begin to act like she wouldn't be okay.

But here I am, on the road to live with a woman I've only met once." Jezereal looked into Gil's eyes to see any source of denial with what she'd said. There was none. Gil was the only person Jezereal really knew in the world. He'd taught her how to fight, hunt, and sleep out of doors, some things with and without her mother's knowledge. Kaylean had cared for Gil every time he'd come by the house, so he was family. Gil felt the pain of knowing

Kaylean was terminally ill. Jezereal, listening to the sounds of the train and one lone voice, her temperament went to annoyance as she heard the father's voice from the train station.

"Mary, can't you shut that baby up!"

"I'm trying, John. He just won't be soothed. He's just tired."

He attempted to whisper, but his voice carried to Jezereal.

"If I throw him off the train, he won't have to be tired of nothing no more. Now stop that hollerin', or I'll give you both something to holler about."

The man tried to thump the baby on the head, but Mary moved, and he thumped her much too hard on the corner of her eye. She winced. He wanted so badly to just backhand her hard again for getting in his way of doing his fatherly duty. Mary buried little Johnny's mouth in her neck to muffle his screams. John felt the impulse to grab and shake little Johnny till he stopped screaming. John knew people were agitated by the baby's crying, and he equally felt they were looking at him because he wasn't doing anything to make the baby stop. If John could throw the baby out the window, he would have. That would be something, for a brief flash in his mind, that would stop their agitation and give everyone some peace, but he knew he couldn't do that.

He was frustrated and felt like he wanted to smash everyone who was looking at him in the face. He jumped out of his seat and spun around in the aisle, "It's you, Mary! You've coddled him too much. If you were a better mother, our son wouldn't disturb all these good people!" He could do that much; he could put the blame on Mary. Surely, the people in the car would be gratified that at least the father of the baby understood their discomfort. He was outdone that they were still glaring at him. He honestly had no idea that even though their nerves were strained by the baby's screaming, they were glaring at him for his belligerence and abuse.

Jezereal felt a familiar heat rising on the surface of her skin. She'd tried to concentrate on ignoring John Sullivan like the others in the car were ignoring the vile way he was talking to Mary. But, she'd heard him, in a whisper, call her a little bitch and say he'd take care of her when he got home. Jezereal was getting angry, but she didn't really feel in a position to do anything to stop it again. Obviously, theirs was a familiar dance. One that had gone on long before she'd shown up in her life, and as soon as they got off the train, the dance would continue. Sure, she could get up and leave the car, stretch her legs, and step out onto the platform for a quick breath of air. But she'd seen enough. John Sullivan wasn't fit to be anyone's husband or father. Jez clutched and repeatedly released the book she'd just opened. She knew this type of man, and she was done with him and his kind.

Gil sat back, feigning sleep; he knew how Jez was being affected. Jez was trying her best to stay out of it and, conversely, knew what was in her heart to do. He felt her body tensing and her breathing getting short. So, Gil made a show of rousing and looking at her like he was coming out of a deep sleep. He rubbed his eyes and stretched, and seeing the book in her hand, he placed his hand over it and took it from her.

"Daily Meditations." He flipped through it and recited:

"May 16. Today is the day that the Lord hath made let us all be glad and rejoice. Well, that sounds about right. Today is a good day, but it ain't finished yet. Give me a minute, and the whole train will know I'm rejoicing on this day."

Jezereal knew from years of experience of feeling that particular itch in Gil's voice that he was about ready to have some fun. They had talked about deep things, and she knew that while he was good at that, there'd always be deep reverberations where he'd feel the need to throw them off...to nullify the feelings.

Because to leave them there, rumbling would make him over-think about all of his own losses and sins. And those led to a place so deep that she knew the pain, so she couldn't stop him from escaping even for a little while. She could turn her mind to her prayer book, sewing, and other people's lives, but Gil had never figured out anything other than drinking and laughing, telling long lies with friends or strangers. In a whisper in his ear, she simply said,

"Gil, don't you dare get all brined up."

Gil simply smiled and looked out the window beyond the other passengers across the aisle seat. He knew what was coming...their old verbal dance.

"You're simply a reprobate, and while I've done this for you in the past when I was too young and stupid to know otherwise than to accept your ways or to do nothing other than drag your skinny butt into a bed, I'm no longer given to throwing a grown man to bed."

"We're on a train, Jez, so that would be a new experience."

"In a bed, on a train, on a rock! It is not, how shall I say, so-cially appropriate, and I'm not doing that tonight, Mr. Gilford!"

Gil only smiled and winked at her. She knew that wink, and Jezereal felt like laughing but stifled it. He was about to say something just as reprobate and consequently inappropriate. She was about to tell him not to even begin his words. But she just shook her head, and he whispered,

"I know what you're thinking; I'm about to say something 'socially inappropriate,' right, my dear? Well, on a train, it might be a little fun for us both if you'd just tuck that Bible in the seat cushion and join the other inappropriate people on this particular train."

He threw a glance at others in their view and those back behind their car.

"Gil, you can make fun of me reading my meditations if you want to. You know I may struggle to know God, but I'm not completely Godless!" She feigned offense, "You've introduced us to these people as kin! The thought of what you're suggesting, even in jest. That's just disgusting."

"No, no, Jez, that's what makes this genius. All the better! Who would think anything of a sister helping her whiskey-soaked brother back to his room?"

She shook her head like he was just a pitiful soul and out of his mind.

"In any case, you can stop right there. I do not have to imagine our mingling, even if the truth were known, because you know the facts of the matter...it won't happen, not now, not in this life, Mister. Just mind yourself."

Gil straightened himself and smiled, kissed her on the cheek, straightened again, and said, while one hand trailed her right cheek,

"Little girl, since the last time I saw you, I've been able to make it to my bed most nights without help."

"Maybe so about that, but know this too; I swear if you get into a fight, don't expect me to get into it...not with my new dress. You'll be on your own."

She had a serious look to anyone else, but Gil knew she'd be there for him if anything went awry...a new dress or naked, Jezereal would fight like a man to save him. Gil winked but didn't promise anything.

Jez settled back into reading her Bible meditations. But, after closing her eyes, she started having memories of her childhood that flowed from memories of Kaylean to before Kaylean—getting hit by just about everyone that owned her, watching her biological mother get battered. Jezereal woke with a start. It was an old dream, just one of many fragmented pieces that disrupted her sleep and were the subject of her daydreams, which she had never been able to make much sense of. But, in them, she stopped whatever went on and is the victor, which, of course, didn't happen for her as a little girl. She stretched her neck and back and allowed herself to flow into the sound and rhythm of the train tracks and the low lighting.

Jezereal's biological mother, Petsy, was a slave. She had been violently impregnated with Jezereal by Petsy's former slave owner. The wife, with only three slaves, Petsy, Old Hank, and Old Thera, was incensed when she realized that Petsy was pregnant. The wife took a fork to Petsy in the kitchen, stabbing Petsy in the stomach repeatedly until Petsy screamed and fell to the floor, begging in whispers for her mistress to stop.

The slave owner's wife realized the fork wasn't doing the job, killing Petsy. So, she grabbed the knife off the table, which Petsy had been using to slice carrots, and launched at her. Her hand was stopped midair by her husband, who knocked the knife out of her hand and dragged his wife, who was still lunging for Petsy, out of the kitchen. He'd forced his wife to take some laudanum to calm her nerves, and after she'd drifted off to sleep amidst fits of weeping and violent outbursts, he sat and pondered what to do. He decided that losing slaves through his wife's murderous ways was a waste of money. He figured he could get something for her before his wife could kill her like she had done a former slave whom he had bedded. Since he was struggling to feed his family and the other two older slaves, he inquired in their vicinity about those looking to buy a woman with a child, but no one had any money or just didn't need another slave. After a week of keeping his wife on laudanum and keeping Petsy in the barn, he sold Petsy for a hog. He was furious with himself as he watched Petsy ride off with her new master. He knew he could have gotten a reasonable price for the both of them if he'd had more time. However, his wife's sister was coming from Virginia for a visit, and it wouldn't do for the situation to continue as it was. The sister was crazier than his wife, and she just might try to take a poke at him herself for disturbing her sister. He wanted no part of that, so what was done was done, and all he could do was return home.

Jezereal had peaceful days as a baby for about a year with the new master and mistress compared to her mother's life with the last. Petsy was allowed to take care of her baby as long as it didn't infringe on her chores and care for the family's needs. Their new owners treated Petsy unkindly, but even though they felt it unchristian to beat even an animal, they had no problem with screaming at her or damning her soul to hell for the most minor of infractions—that is when they noticed her. Jezereal, however, was their daughter's living doll.

She was not allowed to speak to the little girl, only to do as she was commanded. She was dressed up like the doll in the latest fashion but was left without affection of any sort from any of them. She was a doll for the mistress' daughter to play with. If she were at all messed or dirty or not in the exact same condition as she had been left, she was scolded by the mistress, and her daughter pinched Jez viciously. When company came, she was set in a little chair and expected to pose as a doll and act as a doll for hours while the women laughed and admired the play of the mistress's daughter with her doll.

Petsy was much akin to any animal that had been beaten physically and whipped emotionally most of her life. She stuttered and was often slapped for it in the previous family. Thus, she learned not to speak above a whisper, which also incurred disfavor. "Speak up, Nigger!" That would unnerve Petsy, and she'd shout out answers, which engendered a slap for being too loud. She couldn't win for losing. She learned to fade into the background so well that she could be the proverbial fly on the wall. Even the floorboards wouldn't creak when she entered a room. She was, in fact, most times invisible.

White people would just forget that she was in the room. But, for Petsy, even the other slaves would forget she was there. She barely put out any energy that anyone would pick up on or pay attention to, and that's how she survived in the new house. That's why Jezereal could become a doll so easily. Whatever she was as a person, she learned that she could hide it and be someone else for those who expected something else. It was easier to disappear than to take the chance of being noticed until there was a reason to be noticeable upon demand.

When Jez and Petsy had lived with their owners for six years, one night, they heard screaming. They lived in a shack outside of the main house. She started to run toward the house, and Petsy simply put a hand out and dragged her back into the shack. The family, mother, father, and child all died in a house fire.

After the fire, when they could no longer hear any screaming, and the house had burned to the ground, Petsy took her by hand and led her into the night. They walked for days in the woods. Petsy just wandered. She didn't say anything, just walked, no food, nothing to drink, just walking until one day she fell and didn't get back up. Jez, at age six, didn't know what to do, so she sat next to her momma for quite a few days. Then, one day, a man was hunting in the forest. He saw a lady lying on the ground and a little girl lying beside her. He examined the woman and was horrified that she was dead. There didn't appear to be any bodily intrusions. Then he examined the little girl. She was alive! Clearly, she was dehydrated and malnourished. He threw his rifle over his shoulder, grabbed the child, and made his way home quickly.

Jezereal shook her head to clear the memory. She settled back, took a deep breath, and slowly let it out, concentrating at each point on relaxing muscles in her neck, shoulders, chest, and throughout the lower regions of her body. She knew she was getting upset and needed to let go of the anger she felt rising. But she'd seen it before. She'd lived through this woman's pain before, and she wondered if it was just the beginning, the middle, or near the end. Of which she couldn't be sure, but where would the line be drawn? Jezereal remembered the hurt, the pain, and the silent tears. There was no one to tell of their frustration, fear, or pain. No one to stop it. She knew what the final result would be to continue to live with this man.

Jezereal heard the jangling of a door handle attempt to be turned. It wasn't solid and confident. The door half turned, and there was a weight upon the door. The door didn't move. There was a breathy, heavy curse put upon it. The door handle held against the angry jostling over and over again until it finally gave way to the appropriate alignment. When the door finally approved, with excessive force, John thrust forth into the isle. The man to the right of the aisle jumped from his seat, slowly rousing from the previous jostling of the door. John, released from his confines with the forward rush, fell to his knees, immediately comprehending his awkwardness and obviously inebriated; all he could do was curse and laugh. "Shit! Well, goddamn!" He couldn't contain himself from falling, and seeing a grown man leap from his seat, he shrieked, "Mother fucking door!"

As he collected himself and raised up off the floor, he turned to the man. "Sir, I am your most humble servant. Please forgive the most unfortunate arrival. The fucking door! It was stuck. They need to oil the damn thing!"

Jezereal had about enough of this fool. He'd hit his wife once in front of her. He'd threatened his wife and child in front of those in the car. He was cursing and scaring folk, and now he was staring her up and down. She was sick of being around him. So, she tucked her Bible meditations into the cushion of her seat. She stood, looked him long in the eye, raised an eyebrow, and tilted her head just so very slightly, but it was enough for him to get the invitation. She turned and moved through the car out the door until she reached the back of the train.

Alone on the back deck, standing between the angle of the metal rails, she leaned on one side of the rails and propped her foot on the other rail. Sullivan's eyes smoldered, and he rubbed his hands together and smacked his lips like he was preparing to taste something delicious. As he approached closer, she took her foot down, raised her skirt above the ankle, and bent down in front of him. He backed up to get a good look at her, bending over and exposing the flesh from her boot up to her calf. He licked his lips again. Jezereal cringed inside with disgust at that recurring habit. She envisioned kicking him in his face. But, she pulled a thin, flat flask out of her boot and offered him a drink instead. His eyes said he wanted that and more. He took a swig from her flask and reached for her. She pushed him back and tilted the flask back to his lips.

He smiled that a woman would understand him so. She pushed him back into the side rail of the train. She let him grab her by the shoulders and attempt to draw her near. She pushed him back, laughing and continuing to flirt. He went to reach for her but missed. He couldn't see straight. He rubbed his eyes, and within seconds, he stumbled completely into the rail behind him. Jezereal simply walked up to him, placed one hand on his chest, and pushed back on that while lifting him by his feet. With the leverage of the rail, he tilted quite easily, and she flipped him off the side of the train. The train whistle blew as it rounded a bend, and there was a road up ahead. Between that and the lack of stars in the night, she didn't see nor hear him hit the ground. She replaced her flask in her boot.

Jezereal stretched her neck and reentered the train cabin. On the way to her seat, Little John woke up and began fussing. After what she'd just done, she crossed the aisle, took the baby from the sleeping mother, and calmed him, singing, "Hush little baby, don't you cry, Jezzie's going to sing you a lullaby." She gently rocked him to sleep as she walked up and down the aisle of the passenger car.

~ Four ~

JEZEREAL IN MARYLAND

The train pulled into Maryland. The woman waited in her seat for her husband to come back. She figured he was still in the dining car. After the train was nearly empty, she asked the conductor if he'd seen her husband. He said no but that he'd look for him for her. They searched, but no one could locate the husband. Mary became so worried that Jez sat with her to help calm her. She asked, "What's your name, Dear?" Jez was told, "My name is Mary Sullivan. Mary told Jez they were on their way to her sister's because her sister's husband had a work opportunity for her husband. "What has become of him? Did I upset him so much that he got off the train and left us here? How will I make it without him?"

Jez smoothed her hair and told her she would be okay with the Lord, with or without a man, him, or any other one. But, not to worry yet. "He'll probably show up like a bad penny." Mary was caught off guard by the analogy, and there was a hint of a quirky smile and questioning look at Jez, wondering how she knew that had been her life with him. Jez reassured her that everything was going to be okay; she was just talking.

Gil eyed Jez cautiously as they prepared to detrain. He looked at the woman and then at Jez; he shook his head while raising an eyebrow. He knew she'd been up to something. She raised her hands, palms toward him in a motion like it was out of her hands. She lowered her hands, and the look on her face said, "He started it." Gil looked at her and rolled his eyes. She rolled her eyes back.

Jez was ready after she pulled her personal bags together and replaced her meditations into her handbag, refolded her nuts, dried beef, and fruits neatly into different muslin cloths, placed them in her basket, and adjusted her cape and cap. She was ready to detrain. She stood, and as she made final adjustments, she felt a warmth at her side and a not-so-gentle poke. "And you told me not to get into anything. What did you do?"

Jezereal knew immediately what he was talking about. There'd been a quiet confusion amongst the train staff about Sullivan. Mary had been pacing back and forth for the better part of an hour, asking if anyone had seen him. Jezereal had felt more than a minor irritation at why she was asking for a man whose only quest was to make her life more miserable, yet she kept asking for him. And now Gil was needling her in her side as well.

"The *what* doesn't matter if he isn't dead, which I'm sure he isn't; the train wasn't going that fast, he'll come back to his right mind in about a week or so. That should give her time to consider if she'll return to him. I have a little while here to do as I please, and I won't mind talking to her for the week; that's what will please me. Whether she goes back or leaves him, she needs a break!"

"Jezereal Wright, what have you done? In all the things I've ever known you to do, this was not part of it!"

Gil is outdone and in strange territory. Not that he hadn't done or seen many mean and nasty things done to a man, but not from her, his little sister. He thoroughly disapproved of her getting between a man and his wife. "You had no business in that! Always flying high and mighty, gonna get you gone one of these days. Why can't you leave people be? Always messin' in somebody else's mess. What is wrong with you?"

Jez just bent her head to the side and looked at him. He knew that look, that stance. In any case, he surmised from the look, "What's done is done." She'd seen him through worse, so he left it alone. He was left speechless as she politely, efficiently, and without compunction pulled together her belongings, held her head high, approached Mary and her baby, and gave Mary her contact information. She offered her a ride with them into town and that she would pay for their lodging. Mary declined as she wondered if her husband, John, would return for them.

A week or so later, Gil and Jez sat at Gil's elderly aunt's boarding house with whom they were staying. One of the other borders ran into the house with the news of an attack on Fort Sumter, a federal fort that had been taken over by secessionists. They all were horrified that there would be a call to war between the North and South. The people at the house were in an uproar with fear and shock about the affront and a potential call to arms.

It didn't take time for the official call to rally the ranks... At a church picnic of Gil's elderly aunt, a group of recruiters came. They were in fine uniform, and their speeches were riveting.

Gil and Jez both, at the end of the speech, jumped to their feet, applauded the men, and audibly pledged their loyalty simultaneously. Those adjoined, particularly Gil and her aunt, looked at Jez with curiosity. Jezereal realized she'd been inappropriate and sat down quietly, a bit embarrassed.

Gil ran forth with other young men, and the young women swarmed just outside the men. Jez sat in shame and turmoil. She pondered why and how she would fight for the North if she could. It didn't take long to consider that she had been a slave and would do everything possible to stop that system, the wealthy plantation owners and even those that had held her family, although not large plantations. Cotton had become King, and slaves were everywhere. The slaves outnumbered the whites. Jez wondered if that was one of the reasons Kaylean made her get on the train from South Carolina to Maryland. Maybe she felt it coming in some kind of way.

A few days later, in the city center, Jez stood just outside the door of Swan's Tobacconist shop, waiting for Gil. She was actually a bit irritated with him and his pipe smoking. It seemed they were always seeking tobacco in the morning and evening. She'd told him to buy the largest tin possible this time because she was tired of him frequenting the shop with her in tow. But he loved to smoke, and he did look debonair when he smoked his pipe. When he was younger, all he could make work was a corn cob pipe, but now, as a man, he had to sport a much more sophisticated piece of smoking gear. So, she really wasn't all that mad. She was thinking of him, smiling, when movement caught her attention from a side street. She followed the movement and found a regiment forming.

Men were milling around, adjusting uniforms and firearms. It was like her awareness opened up, and she saw others practicing marching. She'd never thought they had to practice in the beginning to know how to march correctly together. She mentally chastised one young recruit who couldn't seem to get his footsteps together. She suppressed an urge to enact it for him. Although it was all in her limbs to do so, she fought it.

"What in the world are you staring at like that? See something you like?" Gil had come up on her from behind. Before she knew she was talking, it came out, "I'd give anything to do what they will do."

Gil stepped back and eyed her for a moment. "Well, not like I wouldn't expect that coming from you. We both know you to try, and you can fight like a man. Hell, we've tussled like brothers on many occasions growing up, but you know I'd never really hurt you like I could have. I know you can take a man down in a fight, but that's if you got the element of surprise and other factors, but damn Jez, there is no way in hell, a woman needs to be in battle like what's coming up. Hell, I don't want to be in it." Jezereal wasn't listening; she was enthralled, and, in her mind, she was already marching and shouldering a rifle.

"Anyway, it's forbidden. No side, North or South, will take a woman into their ranks, so just stop daydreaming. I can see you're gone, not listening, but stop it!" Gil grabbed Jez and shook her till she refocused on him. Listen, what man wants a woman or a child, a momma that's all rough and hard. "You can be a nurse, seamstress, or go find a suitable beau and pine for him and send him love letters to bolster his resolve."

"I can fight, and that doesn't make me roughly hewn," Jez stated. Gil continued talking, and Jez interrupted him, stating she didn't plan to be a wife or mother anyway, so what would be the difference?

"At least on the battlefield, I will know who the enemy is as opposed to one in my own home like the woman we met on the train, Mary Sullivan." She stated with emphasis.

"Okay, that is all fine and true, but Jez, you surely missing anatomy that will keep you from passing the medical examination.

Gil continued to try to get the notion of fighting beside him on the battlefield out of her head. He vehemently expressed, "Have you even heard what I said? Mothers, wives, and sisters are to be protected so they can care for the children left behind. War is not a joke; men are lost and maimed. Who would ever put a woman, the most valuable being on the planet, at risk for losing that nurturing and caring? You are the crucible of God's love, a partner in the creation. We lose the women through this ugliness; we lose all of our lives." With that, he turned and stormed out of the house.

The next day, after Jezereal had completed the last stitches on what she considered some of her best embroidery work ever, It was a simple pattern of green vines and red holly on the white background silk of a matching petticoat and skirt that she would wear to the Christmas town hall ball. She at first had not been in the least bit interested in attending, but Gil had teased her about her lack of social graces, and her aunt had assured her it was in her best interest to attend as unquestionably the most interesting men in the city would attend. In truth, it hadn't taken much teasing or prodding.

As of late, she had begun to tire of being alone or the extra third or fifth of a group. Gil's comments were directed mainly at the fact that she didn't have much patience for a group composed entirely of women. She just wasn't comfortable with idle conversation or given to what she considered frivolous pursuits like shopping for the sake of shopping. Solitary pursuits were a particular favorite way of spending her time, but she also enjoyed sitting in the parlor with her aunt while she read the news, Bible passages, or stories from the prominent writers of the day. But, she was considering now that it might be fun to find out what everyone seemed to be so excited about when in the company of the opposite sex. She'd been in Gil's company her whole life, and while they had touched intimately over the years, neither had ever gone beyond that.

They didn't have that sort of feeling between the two of them. In their last fussing session, she had told him that she didn't want to be married, never expected to, because Jezereal knew she would never marry the one she had loved. Jez remembered Kaylean and herself sewing together one night. Kaylean explained her story of married life to Jezereal before she left home for Maryland. Kaylean never divulged why she married a preacher and stated that it wasn't out of pure love for God or her husband; it was to get away from the life her upbringing had promised. She wanted more out of the life she had known as a child and young woman. So, when she met such a kind and educated man as Joshua, she felt she had done quite well and wouldn't have to suffer as much as before.

After the last stitch, Jez admired her handiwork. She relaxed in her chair and considered her aunt's description of the upcoming ball for the men going off to war and of the young potential suitors who would be in attendance. She imagined them in black tuxedos or perhaps uniforms; even those bordering on general cleanliness levels would all be perfectly polished for the occasion. All white men. She imagined herself dancing and looking into the featureless face of some young white man. As she danced, the young man's face morphed, and she was dancing with a young man quite unlike that who had originated in her vision. She was dancing with Otis. Otis Stratten was a free black welder, and he was well-known in many communities of North Petersburg. Jezereal hadn't heard of him, though.

It was after church services one Wednesday evening when Kaylean and Mr. Northberg were discussing his daughter Lottie's education that Kaylean suggested Jezereal would be a fine tutor. Jezereal had occasionally seen Lottie but had never cared much for her. She was the only daughter of a wealthy man who had lost his wife years before. Jezereal considered Lottie spoiled and unmannered and had no doubt she wasn't doing well in her studies. She winced when she heard Kaylean offer her services.

Mr. Northberg promised a more than ample payment for his daughter's tutoring, and Kaylean countered that it would do Jez a world of good to be of use. He also had an unexpressed hope that Jezereal would rub off on his daughter and that she would become more ladylike and tamer. Jezereal was quiet, though she had always evinced a steady head and an even temperament in polite company.

It was at the Nordberg's when Jezereal first saw Otis. Lottie had been recalcitrant and unprepared for her tutoring. It had been an unfulfilling session on several levels. Frustrated and disgusted, Jez had gone to the well in the backyard for a glass of water, refusing the aid of a slave to bring it to her. She really just wanted to get a breather from her dealings with Lottie. She'd left Lottie in the study and made her way through the kitchen to the outdoors.

She'd smiled as she remembered eavesdropping on Julia, the head maid, a woman she'd often met in town and around the neighborhood. Julia was a sometimes surly thin, black woman with a nervous twitch in her left eyebrow. She heard Julia blessing out Lottie under her breath as she rolled a ball of dough beyond its limit. Julia's arms, though thin, were muscular and strong, and the dough was stretched without mercy under her sweat-drenched shift. Julia caught her breath and curbed her tongue quickly when Jezereal cleared her throat behind her at the kitchen entrance. Julia's eye twitched uncontrollably, wondering how much Jez had heard.

Jezereal wiped a wisp of hair from her forehead and sighed as if she were worn out, which wasn't too far from the truth. She didn't know Julia enough to go too far and commiserate with Julia on the worrisome nature of Lottie. Still, she hoped her action would put Julia at ease about saying anything to Mr. Northberg about what she'd heard in the kitchen.

Jez smiled and winked at Lottie and said, "The air is so hot and heavy today that a fly will work a normal human being to insanity!" "Yes, Miss, it surely is!" exclaimed Julia. "Let me go draw you some cool water from the well." "No, thank you, Julia, I can get it myself. I need some fresh air." She sneaked a quick look back to the study, and Julia got her meaning. "Well, here's a glass for you, Miss." "Give me two, Julia." Julia gave her two figuring; one was for Miss Lottie.

Jez stepped outside, and a hot blast of air met her at the door. "Lord, Lord, Lord, give me some relief from this day!" Just as she spoke her thoughts, Otis emerged from the barn, bronze brown, blackened arms, and muscles rippled as he carried a harness. He laid it on the ground just outside the barn and stood and straightened his back. Jezereal stopped, and her breath was caught somewhere between her thoughts of getting cool water for her and Julia and her body responding in a way it never had to the man moving before her. She hadn't even realized she'd been tracking his movements from his first step outside. She hadn't realized she was taken, mentally savoring his movements.

There had been no thoughts, only sights, and physical sensations. Jezereal was walking when her foot hit a stone, and she twisted her ankle and fell. When she actually began to think again...*What? A rock, I fell, my ankle..*he was beside her helping her up. Her thoughts stopped again, and all she could do was feel and smell. She felt rough hands, one under her right elbow and the other just below her left breast, and they were both pulling her upward. Their pressure was steady and strong, and she felt tiny, weightless beneath them. She was on her feet before her legs were ready to hold her, but he held Jez upright. She could smell his sweat, pungent onions, and iron, and the scent of a man. She remembered Gil's scent and the scent of her father. For a second, she also remembered the scent of another man many, many years before, and she stiffened under his grasp, but this man's scent was different.

Otis felt her stiffen as her feet took hold, and he let her go. She wanted to fall again, to smell him again, but she finally was coming to her right mind and realized that she'd been going to the well and had dropped her glasses in the fall. Jez turned to thank the man without yet taking a look at him. She couldn't yet look at him; her nerves were still tingling, and her legs were weak just from his touch. But, when she turned, she thought herself wholly composed. His eyes knocked everything loose again. Her legs barely wavered, but her heart fell somewhere deep. His eyes were the brownest she'd ever seen, and his pupils were *wide* in the noonday sun. And that's where her heart went into them to a place where a whimper sounded, and it frightened her. She pulled back as hard as she could from that sound. Pain? Pleasure? Stark fear of what she felt made her recoil as if she'd been bitten. She snapped, and where the thank you had formed came anger.

"You scared me!" "I'm sorry Miss." He was surprised by the vehemence in her tone, and he stepped away. Julia was at the door and coming down the steps to intervene. "You alright, Miss Jezereal? Here, baby, give me those glasses, and you sit down here on the step. Otis didn't mean to frighten you. Here, child, let me look at your ankle. Otis, go on. I'll take care of her." Otis tried to offer another apology, but Julia waved him off to the barn. Jezereal could only sneak a peek at him as he bowed his head and turned away. She tried to think of something to say to ameliorate the situation but couldn't. Julia was fussing about her at that moment. She could only observe him now from behind, and even from behind, she felt weak. She allowed Julia to minister to her and hoped it would help whatever ailment she felt.

She was still embarrassed even though he had told her to think nothing of it. He was hurt when he thought he had frightened her. He was working on the bridal out in the yard, and she contrived another break from Lottie just to go out and talk to him. Julia knew what she was up to and merely said, "If you go out, remember Mr. Otis is out there working today. By the way, how's that ankle?" Jez told her she was sure the day would be better than the day before and that her ankle was just fine.

And that was it; Jezereal would go out and get water to cool herself off every day. She was there to tutor Lottie, and he would work on the equipment each day. Around noon, they met and talked for a while when she was getting water, and he just happened to have to work on something outside. Jezereal ran her hands through her hair and pulled at it to feel the strain on her scalp. Whenever she saw and talked to him, she wanted to see and talk to him more. Getting through the time with Lottie was easy then because she could see him. Before him, Jezereal had never thought about a man. However, Otis was all she ever thought about after that first day. She smiled and laughed a lot, more than she ever had or may not ever have again. He was just something so much more than a dream. She'd never had a dream about a man before, and there he was; Otis became her dream.

Otis had been granted manumission, freedom from Old Master Stratten, a slave owner, because he'd been with the Stratten's from birth and had been the favorite of Mrs. Stratten after her only son died as a child. Master Stratten loved his Missus exceedingly, and as she showed much affection to Otis, Mr. Stratten would do no less by him. As it was also under her care, Otis grew in intelligence and social graces. He somehow came to remind his master of himself. Mrs. Stratten had died in childbirth ten years later. Stratten remarried after three years, and the new Mrs. Stratten bore him a son.

While Otis always retained a place of affection in Mr. Stratten's heart, he had moved him to a small cabin with his mother, and there Otis grew to manhood. Because he'd saved up $500 by 21, he paid for his freedom. Otis had been lucky, luckier than most slaves. He had never known the lash or barely a harsh word. He'd learned to read and write and was taught the word of God. Stratten had promised his wife that he'd treat Otis well and teach him a trade, which he honored. At 14, he had commissioned him out to a blacksmith, and he learned the trade and excelled at it.

After Jezereal finished with Lottie, she would take another hour in the evening to meet with Otis and act like she was teaching him to read beyond what he'd already been taught. He was an adept student to learn and out of the desire to please and impress Miss Jezereal. Both felt the uneasiness of their liaison, but neither could impede it, and both ignored the implications. With Jezereal's skin implying that she was a white female and he a black male, six feet five, dark-skinned, muscles rippling, the most handsome man Jez had ever seen, it might be dangerous for them to express their attraction to each other in public.

However, her father, Joshua, had fallen ill, and she had to stay at home in order to help. When Jez told him that she would have to care for her father and that she didn't know when they would see each other again. They both cried in each other's arms and prayed for the day they could find a way to be together.

Jez was lounging in the armchair by the window, thinking about Otis. She had inquired about him but found that he had moved to another state after the deaths of his former owners, who had sold the home. He'd moved out West. She was heartbroken, but what could she do.

It was a warm summer day, yet a breeze came through the open front door. Try as she might to keep her mind on her reading, Gil was moving around upstairs...from the bathroom to his bedroom and back and forth while singing loudly. He was going out on the town that night with a group of his friends. They were to meet in a few hours.

Jez thought to herself, *Really, it'll take that long to get ready? I'll have an episode before then just by him getting on my nerves.* However, she was complaining one minute, and the next minute, Gil was standing in front of her. "Get up, put that book down, and go get dressed. You're going out with us tonight." "What? Ah, I don't think I'm going out with you and your gang of ruffians. No decent woman would be seen with you or any one of them out in public after dark." "Then, it's set. Go get dressed." She had to laugh. He was quick on that one. "Tonight, we're going to the Grover's Theater, and you will see what they say is a fine play."

To Gil's couple of hours getting dressed, it took her about 30 minutes. She sat fully dressed and cloaked when he lighted down the steps, shouting up the staircase that he was ready to go and for her to hurry up. Sitting back in the armchair he'd spurred her out of, she simply said, "What took you so long?"

When they arrived at the theater, Jez looked at Gil and his two buddies...

"Um, this is an opera?"

They fell out laughing... as they had been drinking along the way.

Jezereal looked at them, "You do know, they're going to be talking by singing, right?" she asked apprehensively.

"Yes, yes, we know, but we are imagining all of the pretty women we get to talk to during intermission!"

Jez realized their ulterior motive. "Oh, OK, but you better act right. Don't make me have to punch one of you!"

The opera was starring someone called Vestvali. As they entered the theater, there was much talk about Vestvali. Jez surmised she was a European sensation and had brought her talents to display for America. She listened to the people milling around prior to entering the theater while they were getting seated. From what she learned, Vestvali was a woman impersonating a man. Jez thought *That's weird, kind of sick in some way, not sure I want to see this.* However, she sat enthralled from beginning to end, thinking of life as a game of cards. *Hearts are Trumps* had such a dramatic ending with a grand fireworks display. Jezereal was overjoyed and had an epiphany of an idea. She looked around at the audience. No one else seemed to care that it was a woman acting as a man, and Jez had found the means to her end.

~~~~

Jezereal began following Vestvali on the street, examining her outfit and methods of being a man. Vestvali felt like she was being stalked, but every time she left the theater at night, she could never see anything menacing. But, then, she was a star, so
~~~~

it was possible she just had an admirer. She did notice Jez one day while on stage and is intrigued by Jez's rapture of her performance. She began to notice Jezereal's presence in the plays and then finally caught glimpses of her on the streets near her.

Jez was truly caught up in studying Vestvali's mannerisms."She walks like a man, or very much, I think. She has a free swagger. She throws her leg forth, and her stance is wide. She controls her space. Oh, she's stopping; she's looking at me!"

Jez slinked back, looking for a place to get out of Vestvali's line of sight, and bumped into a wall. There was nowhere to hide. So, she bent down to tie her shoe. Jez kept her head bowed long enough, hoping Vestvali wouldn't notice her. But, no such luck. When she began to rise, Vestvali was still looking at her. Jez knew her predicament; she'd been caught following Vestvali.

Jezereal looked frantically for some reason to be there, someone she could act like she was hailing, something in the street she could pick up, but there was nothing; the street was clean. All she could do was look at Vestvali. Jez's hands dropped to her sides, and she backed away into the shadow of the building beside her.

"You there, come here. Come out of the shadows." Jezereal shuddered; she couldn't be speaking to her personally, could she? She looked around to see if someone near her had attracted Vestvali's attention. "Don't look for someone else. I'm talking to you! Come here, now." Jezereal nearly vomited but quelled the sensation that rose from her stomach. Vestvali evidently meant for her to come out of the shadows. To Vestvali, she was now seen and could do nothing but step forward. Jez had followed her for weeks just to see and watch her, learn from her from a distance, and now she was being beckoned. So, she forced her legs to move forward.

When she was within an arm's distance, she looked upon Vestvali. Her mind switched back and forth involuntarily between looking at a man and knowing she was looking at a woman dressed as a man. She didn't know which to accept, but she was settling somewhere in between. Vestvali was an attractive woman, but she underwent a transformation when she presented as a man. The very features that would make her considered beautiful as a woman were the same features that flattered her as a man. Her face was square, and her cheekbones were high and hollow underneath. It was all in her eyes. Her eyes were androgynous. They were intense but kind, defiant but pained. Her eyes felt everything, but refused entry.

Vestvali was intrigued with the young woman who obviously was interested in her, perhaps infatuated with her. So, one night after her show and Jezereal was leaving the theater, she was asked by the doorman to wait as Vestvali wanted to speak with her. Jezereal almost fainted and had to sit down. Vestvali came out in full array as she left, and on her way out of the door, she turned to Jezereal and invited her to a picnic she was holding the following day. After several weeks of meeting periodically for lunch or dinner, Jezereal asked Vestvali to help her perfect her male persona.

Vestvali was amused and delighted, but she didn't realize Jezereal's motive, and Jez never really told her. They agreed to meet early one morning the following week. Jez was greeted into a very posh hotel room. "Well, here we are, my dear, and I am to understand you want to dress like me?"

Jez responded, "Yes, Sir. Sorry, I mean, yes, Ma'am." Vestvali laughed, whichever is appropriate to how you feel by my presence. I have been dressing like the other for a very long time. So, I take no frontage to how you refer to me. If you forget or don't know what you're looking at, it means I know what I'm doing."

Jez inquired, "How long is a very long time?" Vestvali responded, "Since I was 15." Jez almost jumped, "That is a long time. How old are you now, 40?" Jez said with a straight face, and at Vestvali's feigned look of shock, she winked. "Seriously though, why did you at 15 even think to dress up? What could have made you do that?"

"Well, when you can no longer breathe, and your only true breath must come by being who you really are... it is easy when someone is looking for the old you to go away." Vestvali's eyes closed as she took a long draw on her cigarette. As she opened her eyes, she watched the tendrils of smoke spiral out from her lips and evaporate into the air.

"Although I'm a long way from 40, it has indeed been forever ago." She wiped the corner of each eye with one finger and slowly massaged her nose momentarily before lightly massaging her left temple. She was still lost in the past, and Jezereal sat quietly.

Leaving her thoughts, Vestvali looked at Jez. "So, my dear one, you want to appear to be a man? Let us get to work. Go to my closet and pick out a pair of pants. They should be dark, nothing fancy to draw attention. Look to the far right of the closet. There should be something there to suit your first outing."

Vestvali, in her dressing room, completed her masterpiece, and Jezereal examined herself in the mirror, approving her transformation. Vestvali, standing beside her, turned Jezereal to her, pulled her close, and kissed her. However, Jezereal stood still, neither returning nor receiving the affection. Vestvali stepped away and stuttered.

"Why didn't you return my affection? I'm offering what you obviously want. Surely you know what we are, can be to each other."

Jezereal simply said, "Next time, ask me first."

Vestvali laughed and asked, "May I kiss you, my dear one?"

Jezereal smiled and simply said, "No," and stepped toward the door.

"Good day for now. Thank you so much for helping me. I will repay you," and as a man, Jez raised Vestvali's hand, kissed its back, and backed out of the room with a bow.

Five

JEZEREAL EXPLORES
THE TOWN

She walked out and along tentatively, at first leery of detection and later boldly strutting. She tipped her hat at the ladies and shook her head when they giggled. She got bold and acted like she was going to smoke a cigar. She had tried them with Gil. Of course, she choked on them and never had one after that, but she was perpetrating a façade, and there was no way she'd actually light one up. She was stopped on the street and asked for a match. She stunned herself because she had forgotten that she had to speak as a man. She cleared her throat and told him in a slightly lowered voice that she didn't have any. She summoned the energy not to run but to step around him. When out of sight, she hightailed it to the rooming house and climbed into her room through her back window.

~~~~

Jezereal pondered...What was there to it anyway? Just put on some clothes, cut the hair to the nape of the neck...maybe to a length that could go either way? Then thought... Not really one of those. What was it someone wrote that she read the other day, "Crown and Glory?" The problem was that Jezereal knew
~~~~

the biblical word and was going against it to do as she planned. How would Kaylean have viewed her? Of course, she already knew the answer. Kaylean would shake her head. Joshua would have had a fit. In many ways, they were opposite emotions at different times.

Joshua was quiet and even-keeled, except if one were egregiously offending the Bible, whereas about the Bible, Kaylean was fairly quiet. No, Joshua would have pronounced, "1 Cor 11:14 Does not the very nature of things teach you that if a man has long hair, it is a disgrace to him, 15 but that if a woman has long hair, it is her glory? For long hair is given to her as a covering," and then, he'd have gone onto, "Eze 44:20 "They shall neither shave their heads, nor let their hair grow long, but they shall keep their hair well-trimmed.""

Kaylean actually would have probably thought, "If the girl wants to cut off her hair, let her cut it off. She's the one that has to look stupid, not me." Joshua would have countered that her looking like that did cause them to look stupid. Kaylean would have sighed and said, "She's no different now, really, as when we first got her. If all she wants to do is cut her hair and dress like a man, well, it's better than a number of other things I can think she could get into or do." Or, at least, that's how Jezereal would ideally like to think Kaylean would have responded. It was nice to hope that she'd have acted that way.

Her heart squeezed because she'd never know Kaylean's reaction for sure. Joshua's, she could guarantee, Kaylean's…she shook her head as she stared at herself in the mirror. She missed them both and genuinely wished they were there to yell at her or admonish her to not do what she was about to do with the scissors. Jezereal thought…*Why not just tuck the hair up into the hat and go out?* Of course, she couldn't do that because the stakes, ruse, and purpose were more profound than that.

Jezereal really looked at herself in the mirror and spoke to her inner self. "Jez, if you are going to impersonate a man, you will have to live at it and give up any pretenses. Plus, you can always return to womanhood, which will never change."

Thinking about the other anatomical regions that might be discovered, she understood the others she could transform to a degree. She could certainly lower her voice, but her voice wasn't too feminine in any case. She could ruddy her skin, apply enough makeup from the theater to roughen herself, and work on her walk a bit more. But, in most ways, she wouldn't have to be so obviously male, she thought, as she'd seen Vestvali both ways, and only nuances were different in her character whether she wore a dress or pants.

In general, she felt like a male in men's clothes and a female in women's clothes. She gave off an air of maleness in either, depending on what she wanted the other to feel. Jezereal felt that she could do the same easily. She turned to the mirror, grabbed the hair she usually pulled off to the side, tucked behind her ear, and cut it off above her eyebrows. She looked at herself and stifled a scream.

What had she done to herself? If she kept going, there would be no turning back, and it would be months, maybe a year, before she could look the same again. Was she willing? Did it mean that much to her? She picked up a handful of hair and cut again. Each time, the shock grew less, although she still had a queasiness in her stomach.

When it was all done and lying on a towel in front of her momentarily, she felt like crying. Was she crazy, really crazy? Had she finally gone all the way over the edge? She wasn't sure herself. She heard a step creak outside of her room. Her heart raced so quickly, and her blood surged to her head; she almost fainted. Footsteps passed her door, and she realized Boone, the boarder, was returning for his noon meal. She looked around for something to pull over her head in case the footsteps were real, as they were likely to soon be calling her to supper. Jezereal found a bonnet, pulled it on, tied it, and realized that it would be impossible to figure out an excuse to keep it on her head during the lunch hour, let alone for the remaining hours of the day. She had to get a wig and thus find Vestvali quickly before the noonday meal. As she gathered up her purse, counted the coins inside, and pulled on her cloak, there was a knock at her door. "Yes?"

"Jessie, dear, would you come help me for a minute to remove the roast from the pan?" She thought she'd die on the spot. "Yes, Auntie, right away." She opened the door and swished by her aunt down the stairs to the kitchen. "My dear, I didn't realize you were going out. Where are you off to?" "Oh, just downtown. I wanted to pick up something at the pharmacy."

Jezereal's Fight with Gil

Jezereal was out when Gil arrived. Her aunt was asleep, but the butler let him in. He was told that Mrs. was having her afternoon nap, and Jezereal had stepped out and would return shortly. Gil said, "I'll wait if I can get a cup of coffee." The man-servant went to get him a cup. While he sat, he thought it would be a lark to surprise Jez by being asleep in her bed when she got home. Inside her room, he looked around. "Not the neatest person in the world for a woman, but way better than me." He went to pull his stopwatch out of his pocket, but a coin dropped along with it. Bending over to pick it up, the tip ends of a man's black boot caught his eye.

"What in the hell? Why is there a pair of men's boots underneath little Sissie's bed? Hmm...can it be that she's not so innocent after all? Gil dismissed the thought as she could not quelch his curiosity with a banter of interrogating words and thoughts. So, he laid across her bed and rested.

Later into the evening, Jezereal found Gil sound asleep in her room. Observing him for a moment before commencing to nudge him to wakeful consciousness. Yawning, Gil looked at her questioningly. Then, he stood and stretched, allowing his body to awake from slumber. Being his usual overprotective self-concerning her, he immediately questioned Jez's lifestyle without asking directly.

"I know that you've been around Vestvali a lot. Ah, you're one of those women that like women? Not waiting for her immediate reply, he continues without pause... "That explains it all! Rather than playing the true charade of being a man, you are a man in some way...liking women?"

She merely cocked her head and looked at him until he realized there wouldn't be an answer to any of his questions along that line, true or false. She finally told him, "You know what I want to do. I've been telling you all along. I want to go on the battlefield, too, just like you. Maybe for different reasons, but I have to serve with what I know I can share, do, and you know the other reasons why I have to do it."

He backed up, "Woman, or should I say, man/woman, you've totally lost your mind. I can't take this. Makes me sick to my stomach. All you have to do to serve the cause is be a nurse, a seamstress, or find a suitable beau and pine for him and send him love letters to bolster his resolve."

Jez reiterated their last conversation on the topic. "Gil, because I can fight and ...at least on the battlefield, I'd know who the enemy is.

"You're trying; that's all fine and true, but the bottom line is you are missing a critical part of your body to pass the physical exam, not to mention, I must add- that if you're wounded, you'll be out anyway," Gil stated vehemently, as he turned and walked out. Jez stared at his back without a change of mind with his last retort.

Later that night, Gil returned to visit Jez, drunk, and tried to rip up her men's clothing. He told her, stumbling, "It's an abomination for you to put them on." She snatched a pair of her pants from his hands, looked at him quizzically, and then asked, "Who've you been talking to?" This didn't sound like Gil to use words like abomination.

He shouted at her, "Nobody, I can read the bible. I know what your Daddy use to preach." He begins to quote Deuteronomy. She stopped him. She knew her Bible.

"I know it better than you: "The woman shall not wear that which pertaineth unto a man, neither shall a man put on a woman's garment: for all that do so are abomination unto the LORD thy God."

"So, you know what you're doing. This would kill Kaylean." Gil stated. Jezereal sat down on the bed, loosely holding her pants. She looked far away to where Kaylean was in her head. And, thought, *it would kill her dead...*

Jez gave a false laugh, "Gil, you know she wouldn't be all that angry. She's worn pants in the field while plowing. So, don't even try to bring my mother into this."

Gil cursed her, "You're a mistake in God's creations. You need to go to hell; the Devil is dancing a jig. You're an evil still allowed to roam the world."

Jezereal was so hurt by the curses and vile insinuations. She had to admit to herself that she was afraid for the first time since she met him. He pushed her down onto the bed and held her by the shoulders so she couldn't move to get away.

"Don't make me angry! You're making me angry." He said, looking at her.

Jezereal shut her mouth. She had no alternative in the position she was in. He was indeed stronger than she. As he loosened his grip, she quietly said, "You're scaring me." At that, he got up off of her.

"Well, maybe that's why you are the way you are now. She was a preacher's wife cut just short of the devil then. You couldn't help, be damned. She brought you up from nothing, and that's what you're trying to return to. The Lord struggled with both of you, but you're the most at least Kaylean tried. Wasn't it enough that God gave you another chance with parents like them? Maybe God had pity on yo' po old black soul and gave you better, but you really ain't nothing but a lousy nigger bitch. They should have left you in the ditch where they found you."

Jez looked at Gil... "Oh, brother, you must be pretty drunk to talk like that to me. I'm going to forgive you this one time. Go on and get out of here and sober up."

Gil wasn't leaving... He kept at her... "Did you make love to that woman? Are you a nasty whore for women too? Women, men, it doesn't matter. You really are just like your real momma. Can take the girl out of the filth but can't take the filth out of the girl."

Jez continued to try to denounce Gil's words, and then it hit her... "Ok, brother, you're talking like a damn fool, crazy son-of-a bitch. Oh, that's right, you are a son-of-a-bitch. Stupid son-of-a-bitch at that. Been stupid all of your life. You were stupid when you were born, and your own momma knew it. Your momma looked at your raggedy drunk ass daddy and then at you when she got up and left that moment. She didn't want to stomach a life with two sorry pieces of shit to take care of. Look at you now...stupid and sorry as your daddy ever was. Probably going to die in a pile of horseshit just like him, huh?"

That was it. Their words were so profound and cutting that there was little chance of recovery on either side. As she got to her feet and approached the door, she couldn't help but say, "Guess I am what I am because I grew up with white trash like you."

Gil flipped at Jezereal's words; the sneer on his face turned maniacal, so she dropped him to his knees with an oil lamp beside her on the table near the door. He rolled around for a minute, and as she sat there stunned, she looked at him and wondered how they had gotten there.

A few moments earlier, she'd been happy. She'd greeted him happily earlier that day; he'd been happy. They'd never fought each other; they were there...just five hours earlier. And, now, he was groaning beneath her feet. Five minutes it had only been five minutes since she returned to her room. As she shook her head in absolute amazement, she heard him give a long grunt, and Jez knew that sound; he was in a rage, and she hadn't made a move. She knew she didn't have time to get far. He was mad, real mad, and Jez knew he could hurt her. She couldn't go forward, so she slipped her feet into the seat, jumped off the couch's side, and rolled out of his grasp. She was to her feet as he got to his.

There were no words; neither would get close to being nice. Gil had said some fatal words to their relationship. While stunned, the more she looked at him, the angrier she got, and the very fact that he was moving on her in a threatening manner took him from brother to enemy. That crazy something had unleashed in them. How does your best friend say the most horrible things to you that you've always worried or cringed that an enemy may say to you? How does that friend forgive her or himself for saying it? How do they ever trust each other again? It was the first time they'd ever been in combat against each other.

When Gil woke up the following day, Jez and all her things had disappeared from the rooming house. He looked for her but couldn't find her. She wasn't in the theater. He couldn't find her in any of the stores or their favorite places. She was gone, vanished from his life. And, while he couldn't understand why she was trying to do what she was, he was ashamed of himself for how he'd talked to her and treated her in the room that night. He walked for days, looking for her to no avail. He became so heartbroken that he decided not to enlist in the Union Army. He could only remember glimpses of the fight, and he was appalled that he had so much rage as to fight with her like a man to another man. He'd always cared for her since she was the frightened little girl. He'd broken her trust. He was crushed. He left Maryland and went home to the South.

Jezereal was so distraught that she took a train home to see Kaylean. Horrifyingly, by the time she arrived, Kaylean was on her deathbed, and she wasn't allowed to see her. She stayed until she passed away and buried her mother next to her father. She felt lonely and had to come to terms with her argument with Gil and the part she'd played in it. She wanted to make amends, so she took the train back to find her brother, the only person she had loved in life. But, when she arrived back in Maryland, he was gone. Jez realized she was utterly alone. She considered what Kaylean would say. She'd take it personally and be furious with herself for considering how she might have had something to do with putting such foolish notions into her daughter's head. She'd probably say that the years she allowed, no trained Jez to be more like a man than a woman, were really selfish years, and she had no real plan or abilities of divination to foresee the consequences of that which was now playing out before her. Yes, Kaylean would be worried, but she doubted she'd have done much to stop her.

~ Six ~

JEZEREAL SIGNS UP IN THE UNION ARMY AS PRIVATE JEZEREAL WRIGHT.

Present Day Thoughts

Thinking of her life with the Wrights, the woman felt grati-tude as she had mourned their loss many years ago. Her inner feelings ventured into the understanding of personal interac-tions with people she met after laying both Joshua and Kaylean to their eternal rest.

She got up from the chair, felt her joints, and smiled. Life at 58, her facial muscles that smiled were used more now than in her younger years. The woman thought of her acquaintances after her upset with Gil. Her mind wandered, then lingered longer on Gil. Not wanting to dwell upon him, she cleared her head. She would think about him later and settle on a morality issue. Laughing out loud... she could hear Joshua Wright's voice about her actions. Life as a man...? Jezereal knew she was different. But her reasons were the determining factor that drove her to live beyond the circumstances...

Jezereal found a room in a hotel near the outskirts of the city. In earnest, she began studying the enlistment process. She noticed that no one was asked for proof of identity. Actually, the exams seemed somewhat farcical.

Most recruiters only looked for visible handicaps, such as deafness, poor eyesight, or lameness. Neither army had standardized medical exams, nor those charged with performing them hardly ever ordered recruits to strip off any clothing.

Tacked beside the general store bulletin board extracted from the Boston Journal, Jezereal's breath quickened as she examined the crisp white paper with varying sizes of print announcing...

"More Massachusetts Volunteers Accepted!!!

Three Regiments are to be Immediately Recruited!

**GEN. WILSON'S REGIMENT,
To which CAPT. FOLLETT'S BATTERY is attached;**

**COL. JONES' GALLANT SIXTH REGIMENT,
WHICH WENT "THROUGH BALTIMORE";**

**THE N.E. GUARDS REGIMENT, commanded by that
Excellent officer, MAJOR J.T. STEVENSON"**

Jezereal was drawn to it and became quickly immersed in the next paragraph.

"The undersigned has this day been authorized and directed to fill up the ranks of these regiments forthwith. A grand opportunity is afforded for patriotic persons to enlist in the service of their country under the command of as able officers as the county has yet furnished. Pay and rations will begin immediately on enlistment.

UNIFORMS ALSO PROVIDED!

Citizens of Massachusetts should feel pride in attaching themselves to the regiments from their own state in order to maintain the proud supremacy which the Old Bay State now enjoys in the contest for the Union and the Constitution. The people of many of the towns and cities of the Commonwealth have made ample provision for those joining the ranks of the army. If any person enlists in a Company or Regiment out of the Commonwealth, he cannot share in the bounty which has been thus liberally voted. Wherever any town or city has assumed the privilege of supporting the families of Volunteers, the Commonwealth reimburses such places to the amount of $12 per month for families of three persons. Patriots desiring to serve the country will bear in mind that

THE GENERAL RECRUITING STATION
IS AT
NO. 14 PITTS STREET, BOSTON!
WILLIAM W. BULLOCK,
General Recruiting Officer, Massachusetts Volunteers.

Once she saw this, it seemed she saw them everywhere. Once she read the words "patriotic persons to enlist in the service of their country," she began to imagine herself as one of those patriotic persons. She opened the Boston Journal left on the chaise and saw an ad that said, "GENERAL POPE'S ARMY. Lynch Law for Guerillas and No Rebel Property Guarded!" is the motto of the Second Massachusetts Regiment." It announced that $578.50 would be paid for 21 months of service, and there would be aid for families of four and $125 cash in hand. She didn't really care that much for the money. She had been left well by the Wright family money, and her aunt had cared for her until she married. So, the appeal was purely in serving alongside those who stood against those who were the cause of the horrors she had suffered, and so many continued to suffer under such an unjust system as currently prevailed.

Vestvali stated one night to her, "Well, if you're going to do this remarkably stupid thing, mon amore, you should at least know how to do it right. You'll be wearing it all day and probably night, and for weeks, that is if they don't find you out or you get yourself killed quickly. She rose and removed her shirt. Vestvali looked more barrel-chested than as if she had breasts. She was wrapped well enough that her chest appeared smooth. Jezereal ran her hand across the front to feel how smooth it should be. Vestvali sighed. She knew that was as much as she would get, but she'd derive her own pleasure. Vestvali had her turn in front of a mirror. She put her hands on her shoulders and asked her to remove her shirt. Jezereal did so. Her breasts were small but full. "Now, you'll push your breasts away from the center of your chest (squishing them toward the armpit area) to try to flatten the area around the breastbone. Let's see which way will be best for you. You might do them like this," Vestvali pushes her breasts up and to the side, "Or you might do them this way." She presses them down and to the side.

They chose down and to the sides. Vestvali took her time and pleasure in binding Jezereal's chest. She stood behind her and reached around the front. She placed her left hand to the left of her rib cage and flat against the side of her left breast, right below Jezereal's armpit. "Now, you'll start here. You'll pull it around, high up first and then down, always in this direction. You can lay down, or stand up, however it works best for you to get it on. Pull it tight and keep checking and placing it just so as you go. Once it's on, you can do it like this to hold it in place or not. What do you prefer right now?" She wrapped the bandage in an X across Jezereal's shoulders. "But, that's up to you, depending on how much you need not to show."

When it was complete, Vestvali took equal time to smooth over the top with her hands. Jezereal gave her that momentarily before she bent forward, brushing close to Vestvali, and picked up her shirt. She slid her arms into it and admired the flatness of her chest. She didn't much like the actual feel of binding. She wondered how she would be able to stand it in the heat. Vestvali continued, "Sometimes some bind too tightly. I would advise against that because it can cause you difficulty with breathing and bending and so on. Plus, some men have breasts as well. A chest isn't completely flat, so this doesn't look unnatural under a shirt. I try to put some of the cloth underneath the breast to absorb sweat; you'll need that if you must march long in the heat. Make sure you always keep plenty of water to cool yourself off. You don't need to pass out because someone will be bound to unbutton your shirt for air. When you can remember, put on talcum powder or cornstarch before you bind. Oh, wait a minute, yes. Here, get something like this or like this." Vestvali threw her a thin cotton undershirt and what appeared to be bindings with cloth sewn to it.

"Putting that one underneath it will help. I can only imagine what the field-laundered shirts feel like. I'm thinking, 'scratchy, itchy.' Anyway, you'll use that other one if you find your binding to ride up on you. Pull it down here and tuck the ends into your pants. The most important thing I can tell you, my dear, is to find time away when you can remove it so that your skin can breathe; otherwise, you'll get sores. "Now, you've got this? Shall I show you again?" Vestvali winked and slyly smiled.

Jezereal smiled back and said, "Thank you, Vestvali, dear, but I think I got it the first time."

"No, no, you didn't really get it, but I can still give it to you."

"No, thank you. I'm fine."

"Well, all right if you think you have it down. Let me say, though, that truthfully, many people won't be looking to look at your chest. They do that if they think you're female. If they think you're a male, they'll look at your face, so unless you do something to draw attention to your chest, like get a medal or wear a medal or something, no one will pay very much attention, I'd suspect. Let's see... you'll need some of these, too." Vestvali pulled several long-sleeved, loose-fitting white cotton shirts out of the closet.

"When you can get away but still need discretion, perhaps at night or on a lazy day, you can wear one or a couple of these without your wraps. She had learned from Vestvali how to bind her breasts, when necessary, pad the waists of her trousers, and cut her hair short. She constructed a false mustache from her hair and continued developing a masculine gait. She experimented with how to fake smoke cigars and padded her uniform coat to make herself look more muscular.

> ### Present Day Thoughts
> *The woman summoned memories further into her living the farce of denouncing her femininity, and a name demanded her attention. Alouishes.*
>
> *Enjoying the sharpness of her brain, although her eyes were not so sharp, she sat back down after warming her tea and taking a sip; Mr. Sumersmith was a person of intrigue. His interactions during the period of her life as a man caused her nights of pondering beyond simplistic reasoning, for Alouishes' thoughts were anything but conventional. She smiled as she sipped again at her tea, and the warmth soothed her inner being. She let her mind wander. Alouishes and, ah, yes, Miss Leigh Ann. Jez smiled as the memory nudged toward the forefront of her mind.*

It was through Miss Leigh Ann Samuels that Jezereal met Alouishes Josiah Sumersmith. Although late in her years, Miss Leigh Ann was enamored with Vestvali. She attended every performance. Jezereal had first seen Sumersmith as he assisted his "owner" from her carriage. His steely white tendrils of hair intermixed tousled black curls were intriguing and attractive to Jezereal. She stood in the shadows of an elm tree and watched him as his eyes followed his mistress as she was greeted by fellow theater goers. After she entered the theater, Sumersmith turned around to move his carriage. She stepped out of the shadows, and their eyes met. The golden glow of the streetlight reflected off of his eyes. They were bright brown and intense, his gaze steady. He tipped his hat and smiled directly at her, the smile not a usually appropriate gesture. But he did it, and Jezereal didn't react. She did wonder, though, as to whether anyone else noticed. She glanced around, and the crowd was moving with joyous utterances toward the entry, oblivious to their encounter. Sumersmith broke the connection as he whirled the rest of the way to the carriage, swung a boot onto the step, and lifted himself to the carriage seat. He urged the team forward, and he was gone.

A.J. Sumersmith was an unparalleled, completely unheralded economic genius. He had been thoroughly intrigued with the exchange and use of money from five years of age when, after expending an extensive amount of effort, in his five-year-old mind, carrying Mrs. Jenkins parcels from her former home to the buckboard, she had only given him a penny. In his mind, he should have received as much for his work as the older boy, Samuel, who assisted in the move. Since then, he had lived by the adage to give unto each man his due. "His due" didn't necessarily equate with what you thought the worth of your job was, but paying a man his worth when he had worked for you to his fullest capacity should lead to equitable pay based on behavior. If a man suffered damage to his skull through a gunshot and is no longer able to perform his duties as a manager, but if upon his recovery to the fullest point, he appears able and fulfills all of the duties set forth for him in his new job as a boy in the stockroom, he should be paid a high wage.

Mistaken as he may or may not have been in his beliefs, Sumersmith wholeheartedly believed that economic worth based on mental or physical labor presented an unfair advantage to all human beings...for those who appeared to reap the advantage as well as those who did not. Esteem based on money or material offerings was the antithesis of his moral beliefs.

Although he held no particular religious beliefs and belonged to no certain church, he attended a church service somewhere every Sunday. He often just sat outside the door and acted as if he were attending to something on the ground or helping people in and outside. However, His main concern was just listening to the pastor's words.

Sumersmith was known among many congregations as a kind and benevolent man, if not a bit distant. In truth, Sumersmith watched closely the exchange of money in all his interactions among people. He took a special interest in financial interactions among church members; he learned the lives of people and determined who gave as obligation versus those who gave out of the rewards to be reaped in heaven and those who gave out of sheer innocent love, through ignorance or pre-ignorance. Those who gave because they believed it was the right thing to do for another inhabitant of the planet without worrying about whether or not they'd receive God's graces were particular beneficiaries, even if unbeknownst to them of his kindnesses. He, himself, didn't particularly believe in God, but he was enamored with the innocents receiving a special dispensation in Heaven. So, he honored those low in intelligence and those who had not the ability to judge correctly. Able-bodied and minded individuals who had the ability to reason and only gave to receive were particularly anathema to him.

Jezereal loved Sumersmith from the moment the door opened between them. He was a withered little black man with wildly situated graying black hair. He smiled upon opening the door and then shuffled away quickly as if getting back to an enthusiastically played game in the parlor. She stood in the doorway for a second, wondering what had just happened. Did she miss a greeting and invitation to enter? His smile welcomed her, and he hadn't shut the door in her face, so she assumed the invitation was extended and she was to follow him. She moved through a dark entryway into an equally dark living area and followed a light from a crack in the door that passed through a dining area and a kitchen. She widened the door slowly and found

Sumersmith sitting, legs crossed on the floor, with hundreds of sheets of individual newspapers surrounding him. She eased into the room, "Oh, my dear, what took you so long. I thought you were right behind me." Jezereal was momentarily speechless but stammered, "Well, at the door, I wasn't sure if I had the right person…"

Sumersmith wasn't really concerned or connected anymore to the question he had asked. He was passed that and picked up a paper in his hand, reading it intensely, and then looked up at her. "Did you read the latest on this whole mess?" She didn't really have any idea of what he was talking about. Vestvali gave her his name to talk to if she wanted to know what threatened the Union. "It'd be funny if it weren't so awful. Actually, it is still funny because it's so awful. And it will happen. There is every reason to stop it, but no one who can really. Very few are awake right now. People are sleepwalking, distracted, or stupid. Yes, those three should cover it all. It'll take a hundred years before they become aware of this. It's happened before you know. This is not the first time. Don't believe me. Just revisit the 'Good Book.'" Sumersmith cackled. Jezereal had absolutely no idea of what Sumersmith was laughing about while at the same time sounding as if in despair.

He walked behind a candle, and his hair struck a shadow that appeared wild and animal-like. Because Jezereal was lost in the conversation and couldn't seem to find a moment to enter into it, she stood and watched the erratic movements of his head and hair in the candlelight. The head finally stopped wagging and bobbing, and similarly, Sumersmith stopped talking. Jezereal refocused her eyes from the ceiling above him.

Obviously, A.J. was a man who craved information. He had to know as much as he felt he needed to know about whichever subject occupied his immediate awareness, and those subjects were myriad. His favorite was money. He loved to feel the smoothness of coins in his hand, the weight of it in his pocket, the music of it when shaken. He would count out his coins before he went to bed. The clink of one coin dropped atop another was soothing. He developed a ritual around it. So, he watched intensely anything that affected the movement of money in his life, in his locality, and across the Union. Any information about economics delighted him incessantly.

Although born a slave, he was a Freedman. He had bought his freedom as a younger man through his knowledge of obtaining money, and he managed the release of bondage for others as well. Only his current Mistress knew of his freedman status. He felt it convenient for his purposes to be perceived as a slave. Miss Samuels was a highly respected wealthy dowager. In another city, at another time, she had made money with her body. Sumersmith showed Miss Samuels how to take her money and make it grow. Theirs was a symbiotic relationship, and the benefits were ample. His mistress "loaned him out" to other powerful families in the vicinity. He had been a driver, a butler, an overseer as the part required. His booty was economic information. Jezereal contemplated what she learned from that and consecutive meetings with Mr. A.J. to the point that it took hold of her for years.

~ Seven ~

LIFE IN CAMP AS A SOLDIER

She enlisted on October 3, 1861, and was mustered into her regiment on the 7th. True to what she had learned from her reading and talking to other recruits, she didn't have to take off any of her clothing, and she was quickly processed through the medical check. Once in the ranks, she honed her skills at acting and talking like men. She wore her uniform loose and ill-fitting, and with so many underage boys in the ranks, especially due to their lack of facial hair, it wasn't too difficult for her to pass as a young male. There was actually a young guy that they kept mistaking for her.

A good thing for her was that soldiers slept in their clothes, bathed in their underwear, and went as long as six weeks without changing their underclothes. Many refused to use the camp's odorous and disgusting long, open-trench latrines. Thus, Jezereal did not call undue attention to herself as she acted modestly, trekked to the woods to answer the call of nature and attend to other personal matters, or she left camp before dawn to privately bathe in a nearby stream.

She noted in her diary the lice, the lodgings, the daily drills, the good and the incompetent officers, albeit not by name. She despised the injustices and the treatment of soldiers by unjust, incompetent officers. Still, she didn't speak up to avoid detection. She worked in a passive-aggressive way to affect small justices in the camp. Jezereal went to sleep, nights upon open hard ground. No trees, no tent, and no blanket to encourage sleep. She was so tired that she didn't even think about that. She just laid down and let the night have its will.

When she arose the next morning, she actually felt refreshed. No bad dreams, no aching limbs; she just woke up a bit startled that she hadn't taken much care to consider the surroundings of where she slept. She, with her hands, absently, surveyed her body. She found a tick at the base of her scalp and pulled it off. While considering how deeply she had slept and examining the landscape around her, her fingers roamed her arms, legs, and torso and found risings from various mosquito bites. She scratched at the bites on her wrist and face while considering where she was and what she was to do next.

When she first entered, she often merely read letters, newspapers, and her bible to pass the time. And, while other soldiers read their bibles as well when they started calling her preacher, she put away actively reading her Bible in front of others. She couldn't afford to be known or tagged as anyone to remember. She started writing letters to Gil:

"The loneliness is what gets me. I've never felt lonely, Gil, because I always knew you and momma were here for me. But, as I sit here with all hell breaking loose and I can't do anything seemingly to stop it, I just want to see you, hold you, see momma, hear her laugh. Touch somebody who makes me have a reason to continue with all this. I know I've always been somewhat "weird" to people, stubborn and headstrong to those who knew me best, but quiet and receding to those who didn't, but

the two of you took me out of a dark place, a very dark place, where there was no hope. No thought or hope to survive where I'd been, just an animal instinct to live on. When you met me, so little as we were, I was not connected to the human race.

The "humans" I had known before Momma and Daddy took me in were horrible, ancient beasts from out of the Bible...Behemoths and leviathans. Why would the Lord let these beasts roam upon the earth and do such terrible things to people? I struggled with why he didn't care about me. He made them, and he made me, too. Why? I guess my mother and I were just in their way. I don't mean Kaylean. I mean my real momma. I hurt for her so much sometimes that it makes me quite mad. They beat her down so bad, scared her so much, and made her have no hope at all in life that the only spark she had for me was to maybe see me so small as maybe a little worse off than her. So, something in her had to rise up and protect me.

There wasn't much she could do, though. The best she could do, and I don't fault her for that in any kind of way, is to drag me out from that place where she existed in turmoil and pain and throw me beside the road. I was so little, so beaten and hurt down there, that I don't even remember my momma saying goodbye. I'd like to think she kissed my face, then held and rocked me long, but I don't know. ...I don't know what my last hours or minutes were with my mother. I don't know...she's dead now, out of pain and misery from my "God" who let loose the beasts upon the earth. How do I not have a bad feeling about this "God"? How do I understand how He could, in his "love," let this happen to an innocent woman? I know the Bible by heart, but, yet, still, I don't understand. I wish I could throw my Bible in the fire and let it be done. Understand it? All I can do is find my space on Earth, now, I think. Stop those who would perpetuate evil who are within my grasp. "

In another letter, she wrote to Gil to be sent to his home, not knowing if he was there or where he was. In retrospect, she questioned the life she had chosen, being sure not to include anything that could be found out about her true identity, and then talked about the hardships. She described her fears of battle and what she would face in the stirrings of battle the next day.

> *"I've seen strong, cocky able young men, filled with glory, go out to battle, and I've seen them return. I now understand there's a difference between a skirmish, an engagement, and a battle. There's exhilaration in the men's eyes after a skirmish. There's still a feeling of victory, yet fear and fatigue after a skirmish, and then after a battle, the men are changed.*
>
> *It's quiet after a battle. We all can't half hear; many with shaken nerves, but for most, there are few words. Can't hear them anyway. Those men are "touchy," and any wise person has long learned to leave the newly initiated into battle alone." I could walk away. No one would know. But you may be fighting somewhere, and as long as you fight, I must fight as well."*

Jez thought of her letters to Gil and repositioned herself to rest her eyes as much as any soldier could...

First battle

The regiment had been informed that a battle would ensue the next day. Her nerves were strained all day, and she had no ability to eat. Jezereal kept trying but couldn't hold even a morsel down. As she lay there that evening, she pondered what it would feel like to be wounded by a bullet or being stabbed or trampled. But, she was not alone in her fear; it could be sensed throughout the regiment. At dawn came the call to march, and her legs felt weak, and she felt barely able to move, but through sheer will, she forced them into the step of the march. At first, the march was long, tiring, and monotonous, but as they approached the line of battle, anxieties soared due to the look of terror in others' eyes and her efforts to suppress a similar look in her own.

She tried desperately to listen and take heart and refuge in her officer's words of "an assured victory for the Union". However, for her, there was a general sense of not being able to hear or remember much. She approached the line of defense with the same shakiness that'd accompanied her on the road. She went in and out of the process until, at some point, something flipped inside of her, and she finally connected with the familiarity of fear in her life.

The hours spent digging in gave her something to do and to concentrate on. She didn't have to think; just dig with the short and shallow trowel given to all. She considered why they didn't have bigger tools, but after a while, the monotonous digging gave way to a rhythm, a calming peace. After a while, it was clear that nothing would be happening immediately or even that day. Jez felt the need to be clean before battle...perhaps somehow to be clean in body, at least before she potentially met her maker. To clean the spirit would have probably taken more. She couldn't really repent of much she'd done in life because she wasn't particularly sorry for anything so far. Just on some level, she needed to be clean. Maybe it would help the Lord recognize her.

She stretched out by the riverside and dipped her hand in the water. She bent forward and submerged her face in the waters of her cupped hands. She thought, "Today, Lord, I commend my spirit." Her hands shook, and she barely had water to put her face in. When she could do no more, she sat back.

"A worthy try and valiant effort!" A voice came from behind her. She turned. It was Grisly Grisom leaning on his rifle, his eyes steady and serious. "I've been watching you calling on the Lord." She wondered if he mocked her, but nothing in him seemed to be laughing or taking delight. If he had been mocking her, she would have held no defiance because she would have mocked herself. "Boy, maybe he heard you say enough to include all of the rest of us. I don't know about baptizing yourself, though. I think you need a preacher for that." She smiled at that, and he smiled. "Oh, I was just trying to clean myself."

"That's what baptizing usually means too. Either way didn't look like you could hold much water anyways. By the way, to-morrow, don't drink too much in the morning. Pee as much as you can tonight. Your first battle, you don't know how you'll be. But, ain't nothing nice about pissin' allover yerself."

Jezereal took that as gospel and didn't drink too much that night or the next morning. She'd have to be sure to pee early, as had always been her practice. He stood up straight. Picked up his rifle and already deep again into his own thoughts, he strode on down the riverside. She wondered where he had gone that quickly. Hours later, with light in the sky returning to announce the next day, lying in wait for the next order—the call to battle, she listened to those in the trenches with her, and she learned why they felt the need to fight. Some fought for glory, some for the Union, some for money to feed their families, some for adventure, and some for God. She was intrigued by the latter as she thought, "God can kill for himself. He doesn't need you." She and those in her regiment waited on the side of the road.

The four-man rank had split into two on each side so that am-munition wagons could move to the front and off to the left fork to prepare their place for the battle. Jezereal felt her stomach quiver. It was evident everyone's nerves were on edge. It didn't help that an even more jumpy soldier tripped on a rock and discharged his weapon. So, many others started shooting at trees, rocks, and other natural structures to kill the sniper who had attempted to cull their column. Cease-fire had to be screamed and almost slapped into some of the poor boys who were filling the unoffending landscape with lead balls. Jezereal, upon hearing the rebel yell and the call to charge, charged with a scream so deep she marveled at its viciousness and then screamed all the louder. Once in it, there was no thinking, no questions, no wonder at her actions, no fear. She fought. Men were falling all around both sides.

Jezereal had been pinned down for hours. There was no going forward and no retreating. There was a battle to the left of her and to the right. There had been so much fire from cannonades and rifles for those hours that her nerves became frazzled again. If it was a cowardly act to merely stay put and not move, whether by order or inclination to glory, she wasn't the only coward. Men lay behind rocks and logs everywhere that she could see. No one moved very far, and she imagined there was just as much terror and indecision emanating from the field that it paralyzed even the wind because it was hot and miserable lying there. There was already no help to be given to the brethren in front of the field.

The Rebs had dispatched with them almost as soon as they'd arrived on the scene. Jezereal could hear the moaning of young men in blue, but she also suspected much moaning was happening for both sides. She wondered if she would have the courage to get up again or if she would just lie there. After all, after the battle ended, as long as she wasn't captured, she could easily fade back into civilian life and leave Private Wright a deserter or dead for eternity. Maybe she could write to the government that she'd found him wounded and that he died honorably and was thus buried in a cemetery along some unknown, unnamed road. That'd be easy enough either way it went. She just had to get out alive. Bits of rock sprayed from the rock she hid behind, and she clutched herself as tight as she could to keep all body parts behind it. When the spraying continued as if the sniper were trying to chip away at the rock bit by bit, she just couldn't take it anymore and drifted off to sleep out of no will of her own.

Several battles later, Jezereal walked through a field of dead and dying. She was exhausted. She knew she was moving, but was having real difficulty focusing on any particular thing. She didn't like the feeling. She shook her head to clear away the disconnection, the fog. She considered... "Many good lives were lost today. Most of all were men, but there were some like me. I could swear I looked into the eyes of another woman today. I'm sure she was. But, she went down in the first wave from what I heard happened to her regiment. Ah, Jesus, some were children, teenagers, maybe not even past 15 good. How in the world did they get enlisted? How could they lie well enough to be taken seriously? Guess they could say they're 18. Nobody cared, though. All believed that they were doing what was right to do. So, all went home to heaven, maybe."

She kicked and stepped over something burnt and black mixed with red in her path, and only after she was over it did she turn to look at what she'd stepped over. She ran a roughened hand over her brow, and the scratch of her own flesh against her flesh cleared the way to a thought. "That was a body you just stepped over..." She stopped and contemplated that. "Death is nothing really, is it? Why doesn't it look like anything anymore? The body is about as interesting after the moment of death as a cord of wood. It'll be grotesque within a day, bloated, blackened, foul from releasing bodily fluids and refuse, an object of disgust. I suppose that is a truly terrible thing for a Christian woman to say, but it is how I have often felt. And after having seen so many, it is nearly impossible for me to feel otherwise.

The only thing of interest that appears to have some effect when I see a body lying on the ground is what color is its uniform. How utterly dreadful that thought is, the thought of wanting to kick a body as I pass to the point of doing and not even knowing it. Yet, on the other hand, to waste the energy to do so is equally awful. After all, it was a human being." She thought to herself, "I once kicked a body clad in grey, and it groaned. That groan took me by surprise, and I jumped away from it. I searched around where I stood and found a large stick. I wasn't going to risk bending over and touching or turning him over lest he be in a frenzy and shoot me. I couldn't see his hands, so who knows what he might have hidden from my sight. I lightly tapped him upon his head with the stick but smartly enough for him to feel it.

'Mister, are you awake?' He was silent. If he were awake, he'd have realized his predicament. Face down, he wouldn't have been able to see her face and to discern if at all possible if I were friend or foe. His thoughts were probably swiftly pursuing which course of action to take. I figured to put him at some rest and save myself a fight. 'Look, Mister, I'll not harm you if you'll not harm me. Let me help you if I can. Say or do something to let me know you want help from me; otherwise, I'll walk away now and leave you to your own providence." Shortly came another groan less heavily laden with misery than the first. It was more of a sigh of resignation and a request. It must have been a relief to hear a woman's voice, particularly one offering aid.

Jez stooped and grabbed one shoulder and, with some effort, could roll him over onto his back. He, barely conscious, grimaced in pain. "Ah, sweet Jesus!" she almost screamed. He was no more than a boy, maybe 16 or 17. How he clung still to life with two holes in his chest was something she'd wonder about later. She knew there was naught to be done for the boy. He never actually opened his eyes, but somehow, as she lay beside him on the ground and wrapped her arms around him as much as she could, the air around them felt calm.

She stroked his face and sang "Carry me home sweet Jesus" and then "In the Arms of Our Lord." Quietly, peacefully, as she sang to the young man, he went home to our Lord. She thought about how strongly we fight and wail and beg for a soul to stay in someone that we love and care about and just how futile an effort that is. The ghost can no longer be grasped, held onto, or cajoled to stay in one place by another human being than one can lay hold to spark off a fire.

She lay with him a few moments more, asking our Lord to welcome the youngling back home to Him, knowing fully God would be merciful and accepting of his soul. She thought to herself, *All of us have perhaps done tragic, sinful things in this unholy war, and I beg you, Lord, to spread your love and forgiveness freely amongst those of us destined to meet 'You' this year and those to come.*

She sat up and was compelled to examine his face. "He not all that handsome, especially like this. Fairly common to look upon, but I definitely would have danced with him if he'd asked me at a social gathering. In his uniform, he'd have a bearing of dash. He was obviously cut off from his troops, perhaps on his way back home or to the battlefield, but cut down from a Union bullet in his tracks. Several, probably at once, took the time to target him with their bullets. Had he been of good cheer or evil vicissitude? Either way, now he is gonna be just bone soon." Sticking slightly outside his jacket was a white envelope. She pulled it out, and it read to *Maraleigh Trowbridge.*

Mother, wife, sister? Jez thought to read it. Perhaps it would have given her a glimpse of the type of soon-to-be, considered man. A sense of who the young lad was- that had just felt his soul go to glory. But it didn't matter. She had no real need to know; there was a sweetness in not letting him die alone. You could say that her foot was directed toward him for some reason. After that, she stopped kicking men out of malice. That never happened again.

She once saw a bird perched upon the forehead of a dead body. It was fit and unfit for it to do that. Fit as the body moved no more and probably felt no different than a broken tree branch. Unfit as that bird should have had the fear of man in it, whether dead or alive. But in those strange days, with so many cords of wood littering the countryside for days before they were removed, even the birds forgot which was which and what they should be afraid of. She had to ride through the area quickly after that. It struck a singular horror in her mind that perhaps a bird carrying away a meal of flesh would drop a piece of some decaying body upon her head. She had to shake away the thought. *"Ridiculous, I know; birds don't have a predilection for flesh, but I can't get that out of my head. A shred of red flesh landing upon the whiteness of my blouse or hurled from the sky to slap upon my cheek, leaving a long red stain down the side of my face. No, no, no!"*

Back in a camp

Jezereal moved in step, more like a side shuffle, with the men in the mess line. This evening, they had pooled their food together and decided that maybe with many different pieces, they could get a good stew. She was wrong. She suppressed the urge to gag at the food slopped in her mess cup by the cook. Perhaps it might have fared better in more able hands than he either elected or offered to cook.

She frowned visibly at the hurried swirl of fatty salt pork pieces and supposed vegetables following behind the pork's movements. It wasn't like it was unusual for her to eat a maggot or two at least early on, but she was pretty good at least looking over her food quickly before consuming it. While still in step, she focused a moment to attempt to identify the vegetables. Cabbage leaves, turnip tops, slivers of carrots, and maybe even an onion were barely identifiable, but that was more than she could do with any of the other subjects floating in her cup.

She mentally shook her head at the particularly non-delectable main fare she now carried for her evening meal. She ate it, though. She learned well that you eat when something edible presents itself because it may be a while before anything better comes along. These were the lean years further into the war. So much had been destroyed or used from the land and farms that resources were lean all over the South and would only worsen if the infernal war didn't end.

A young newcomer shuffled along beside her in line. His uniform was only just acquainted with dust and mud. It had not yet been addressed by the relentless unfavorable conditions of infantry life, or even blessed days, if any. She felt compassion mixed with irritation. She had watched him in camp that day and now, in the mess line. She was summing up and reckoning with his will and spirit in combat, and he wasn't faring well.

"What is this...? He made the mistake of bending to sniff the contents of his can. "Oh, God!" and he gagged once and then again; with the second one, he reeled away from the chow line, not making it very far before the entire company witnessed his sensitivities. He made an audible, physical expression of his disgust. His neck muscles strained, and his jaw jutted forward and "hurrahed," which many of the seasoned soldiers in line shouted with each of his expressions of the contents of his stomach.

Jezereal eyed him with interest, wondering what it would take for him to become a hardened warrior. A delicate stomach

is more often than not seasoned through prolonged marching, camping, and combat if one should be blessed to live
through those requisite experiences to get one to that point.
She shrugged her shoulders, and being nudged to continue by
the next man in line, she shuffled away from the line, meal in
hand, thus shutting down her mind and heart to that young
man's future. She had other things to contemplate that would
hopefully prolong that young man's destiny.

Three days later

Jezereal was a soldier. She had stood in battle and been
bloodied, some of it her own, much of it others. She'd heard the
whizzing of the mini balls past her ear. As deadly of little things
as they were, they'd soon learned to discount their significance
as if fanning off a mosquito. Certain parts of what was once a
civilized life were fairly off the charts during that time. Things
had to be made to work; however, someone could think or know
enough about the terrain or conditions to make them work.
It was hard to find food at times. Jezereal learned the pain of
blisters from the marches and ill-fitting boots. She felt similar
to the frontier men and women she read about, and she had to
survive like them. It had become a wilderness, and they all had
to, at some point, figure out how to survive the lay of the land.
They had to learn how to work together and improvise when
rations, equipment, and clothing were short. Nothing fun about
any of that. Jezereal's regiment returned one morning from
exercises. As they walked back in, she looked over to the side
where women were doing laundry and laughing with some men
who had made it back before her.

She had to blink and wipe her eyes. Was she seeing who she
thought she was seeing? Lo and behold, it was none other than
Mary Sullivan. Mary was working as a laundress for the Union

cause, which, unfortunately, was also considered by some as a euphemism for a prostitute. Jez gasped, got herself together, pulled her cap low on her head, and approached her. She had to learn if it were true for Mary. It was, and her son clearly wasn't with her; where could he be? How had she gotten there? Jez stumbled back to her tent with her mind whirling. "Oh, my Lord! Did I do this to her? Was I wrong in tossing him off the train? Did I injure or kill him, or did he just run off? Maybe she and her son would have been better off with him than what she's living like now. I thought I was helping her, the baby, and the Lord was correcting him. But who was I to do that to someone I didn't even know. I am so sorry, Lord, if I did her wrong, and please, let me make it up to her one day."

Jezereal couldn't rest peacefully, well, not as much as she could at any other time under the circumstances. Maybe she was wrong; she was simply a hired laundress who had wandered into the wrong section of the camp. Or, maybe she knew one of the women on that side. After all, all the women engaged in laundry work by day, but seeing her wander that way towards the end of the evening gave her cause to wonder. The thought of Mary living her life now as a "hooker" nagged at her. She'd seen women and men in the brothels of New Orleans, D.C., Memphis, and various other ports. She couldn't understand how she could have ended up there if John had made it home. John was enlisted in their regiment and definitely wasn't in their camp. Her only surmise could be that it was because of her. However, as she finally drifted to sleep, Jez would have to somehow ask Mary herself how she'd come to be there.

The next morning, as they were reading themselves to practice maneuvers, she passed by Mary. She slowed her approach. Just as Mary turned in her direction, she winked at her and asked, "May I have the pleasure of your company this evening?"

Mary dropped her eyes quickly, out of surprise, and then raised her eyes to Jez's and said, "Yes, of course." Jez nodded while stifling the urge to wince.

Later that night, in Mary's tent, Mary sat on her cot and began to undress. Jez stopped her hand and said, "Oh, no, Ma'am. Not that tonight, I'm sorry; I just want to talk to a nice, pretty lady. It gets so lonely out here. You spend your time drilling, practicing, and listening to other men. Sometimes, you just want to talk to a woman. You know what I mean?" Mary took her hand down from her chest, sighed almost as if in relief, and whispered, "Yeah, I do." Jez sat down next to her and began to complain about camp life, how she missed her family, how she longed for the war to be over so that she could go back to the life she had before the conflagration.

Mary listened quietly, also seeing her life before. Jez turned to her and said, "May I ask what your life was like before all of this?" Mary looked away from him, pulled her knees to her chest, and wrapped her arms around them. Jez put her hand on her shoulder, "No worries, it's been hard for us all before and now, and who knows how long it will be for life to return to some semblance of before or maybe something better than before." They both sat silent, and then Mary spoke quietly, tears coming to her eyes, "I remember some parts of my life in Ireland, but not much. My pappa brought me over here when I was about ten after momma died. He wanted a new life after the famine and momma gone. It was a struggle for him, and he gave me away when I was 16. I was married for two years.

Guess I wasn't a good enough wife. I let him do whatever he wanted; he was my husband... He just up and left me for another woman. Left me with a baby...such a beautiful baby. Left me with nothing, but my baby." She held her head back and cracked her neck. "I had nowhere to live, no money to return home, no friends to ask for help. Nothing." She bowed her head, and her body began to shake. "Even my baby boy left me." She pushed her shoulders back, took a deep breath, and said, "He died of the flu in my arms." Jez wanted to console her and reached to stroke her face. Jez told her, "I'm sorry." Mary pushed away his hand, "No, I'm worth only one thing now. I don't want to talk anymore."

Jez started to ask how she could help her, but Mary held up her hand, "Please, leave." Jez rose and backed out of the tent. They hadn't even exchanged names. Jezereal shook her head on her way back to her tent. Questions careened through her head. "What did the women in the camp have to deal with from the other men, some of them deadened inside!? What about the boys that were just being initiated into the world by others than their mothers and sisters? How would this change them? No matter how kind or demanding mothers or sisters were, their first introduction to other women now are the prostitutes of war?

Were those without some sort of religion doomed to suffer until they found a woman or man to teach them a straighter road? A path to a place they had perhaps never been before?

All she could think about as she drifted off to sleep was, "Eat, drink, and be merry is the battle cry in this war. Food was becoming scarce and in between. When there is, the drink is plentiful except if some temperate leader makes it not. And, merry, well, merry can obviously include so many things. And, in war, merry was being taken to a great advantage.

Present Day Thoughts

Times have changed and resonated within her as she awakened from her rest. She heard a ruckus from outside, and she heard a thump. Rising to the occasion, she walked to the window and peered out. A raccoon had tumbled over a barrel.

The barrel, once closed, the lid fell away, creating an opening. She watched momentarily as three more raccoons came into view, and they all went in. Shielded against the back of the barn and the barrel opening close to her fireplace exhaust, accommodations made in nature were given. The world has a way of caring for its own, although not always as resourceful nor allocating as the raccoons in the barrel. The government... makes a layman sigh with annoyance.

One evening, sitting at camp, Jezereal heard two officers whispering in a tent about how the government had been re-cruiting people for espionage and countering the foes lurking in their midst. Evidently, one agent had found that individuals from both sides were making exchanges that were problematic to the Union's cause and, thus, illegal. She returned to her tent and soon made her way back to Sumersmith for his consider-ation of what she had learned. She had to talk to Sumersmith. Sumersmith sat and shook his head slowly at her as if she were a child, and he was tired of saying something over again. He told her, "It's not the paper to follow; it is the source of the paper itself. Or rather the 'cloth.' Can you hear me now?"

From then on, Jez followed the cloth, which led her to the money. She found men supplying the Confederacy with Union goods and those in the Union supplying the Confederacy. Sumersmith's words began to become reality. To buy cloth in the Union cost about three times as much as it did to buy cotton/cloth in the South. So, it was a "scratch my back, and I'll scratch yours" kind of thing, and they all were making money. She turned in her reports. They then put her on money counterfeiting, which she knew nothing about, but she learned. Counterfeiting had come about when they put the money on paper, so while she was tracking both the "money" and the cloth, she came to find out there were people who had figured out how to fake the money. Fake money was flowing between both lines. She just had to shake her head and how wily people could be. She was able to send information regarding some that led to counterfeiting busts, but nothing substantial; however, she was astounded that some counterfeited bills were excellent pieces of workmanship.

However, as she delved deeper into the understanding of counterfeiting, she began to see some things that she felt a deep desire to ignore. She began to "see" things she hadn't before at work in the Treasury itself, which were potentially licentious behaviors. Her informal investigation revealed that they were buying equipment for enormous amounts of money that were impractical and worse than the original equipment, but from which friends of the Treasury benefited. She hadn't been asked to make such a summation. Still, she sent a note of the possibilities to Baker, Civil War investigator, and he invited her to the White House.

~ Eight ~

PRESIDENT LINCOLN

Present Day Thoughts

The room grew chilly as the woman woke from her slumber. Walking to the logs and upon the ambers of the fire, she poked the log, positioning it; the fire caught, and she felt the heat. Looking out the window to the orange haze of the sky as the sunset low beyond the trees, the brilliance of the last of the day's light glistened upon the earth's white blanket. The gleam of the day ending brought memories of her birth mother. "We, the people," she said aloud. "Hmph," she said as she stretched upward from the bent position. Her life, like her birth mother's, was not her own... Life has a way of bringing your past experiences to your present day. Spirits be damned, she thought, thinking about how strange her life started, looking around, taking into account all her life actions in a fleeting moment. "Experience is the best teacher," she quoted, realizing she was speaking to herself as she heard her own voice.

She chuckled at the memory of her service to President Lincoln and his call to duty, as some things are not always as they seem, her memory a little fuzzy.

She pushed her feet up and down upon the floor, and her chair rocked back and forth as her mind wandered. Her continued life as a man intrigued her, as well as all she had accomplished.

Investigator Lafayette Curry Baker meets Lt. Wright

Baker recounted a conversation he had had with the president. "Jezereal, according to the President, we have a pretty big army already on paper, but what we want is men in boots and breeches. This great array of figures, with respect to soldiers, will not suppress the rebellion. I want men who can carry muskets and eat hard-tack. We need men who are fleet of foot and willing to go beyond the wars of the field."

"We need to know what's going on before they get out of there. As you've already expressed a desire to see beyond the lines, let me say that you are who I'm looking for at this time. So, I accept your request to be an agent. Let me get back to you tomorrow." Jezereal had to calm herself down as she listened to his thoughts.The next day, she was called back to talk with Baker. He ordered her to go into disguise to catch bounty jumpers. She knew exactly what he was asking. He wanted to do away with men who enlisted with either army off and on to get the enlistment awards and then desert it. These individuals couldn't be counted upon, and he wanted nothing to do with them and the Union.

Meeting President Lincoln

There was no grand announcement; the President was ready to give her an audience. Jezereal arrived early to meet with Baker and was told that President Lincoln was expecting her and to have a seat in a lush chair outside the President's office. Not more than five minutes later, the door opened, and it was President Lincoln himself who greeted her and invited her into his chamber. "Hello, Lieutenant Wright." President Lincoln extended a long hand attached to a long arm, which led to broad shoulders that supported a long neck, then to a long face. Jez's thoughts fluctuated about the man she was in front of and the pictures she had seen of him. Having Lincoln in front of her rendered her speechless. Jezereal just smiled, extended her hand into his, closed her eyes, and nodded. She was in the presence of "Mr. Lincoln," whom Sumersmith had already schooled her on how he'd gained the presidency.

"Just by a margin," Sumersmith stated, "because all the other parties were so sure one of them would gain it, that it broke them down along so many different party lines, that he slid through with the vote to the presidency. It could have gone so many other ways if those in the race had been savvy and less self-assured.

Baker stood by to hear her presentation to the president. Oddly enough, Lincoln turned to Baker and said, "Thank you, Baker. I can handle this from here. Standby, though; I will need you in about 30 minutes or less."

Baker was taken aback and not particularly happy thinking about what he would later have to ask Wright and what his answer would be.

In any case, he left, and Jezereal and the President settled into their respective seats across from each other. He asked her several questions about her life before the war. She lied, of course, only in the respect of talking about her same life, but as a man. He let it sink in. He asked her what she saw when she looked at him.

She smiled and said, "Mr. President, I can say many things about you in terms of what I've heard. However, being around here and now with you, I think there are some things no one will ever know or comprehend."

He nodded. He had no idea she had been listening to his undertakings with the Spiritualist. He turned in his chair and looked out the window, and considering her words, he uttered, "Some of which will never be known. I guess that's a good thing. I wonder who I'd have been had I not gone into politics."

He stood and said, "OK, private, can you? Are you willing to help save the Union?"

She stood, bowed her head to him, and said, "Yes, Sir, very much so."

He gave her a confidential assignment that was between the two of them, not to be expressed to anyone else. She felt so divided between getting to meet and know President Lincoln and her assignment from Baker to watch him. Of course, she stopped by Sumersmith's and told him most of what had transpired, not mentioning her assignment per se from Lincoln in real terms. She confided that she might be going into agent work for the Union. He laid back on the floor and looked at the ceiling. "You're just taking a step toward your ideals to help make things right. However, my dear, nothing will happen of it."

Jez exclaimed, "Surely you jest, of course, at some time they will prosecute these people. They may be clearly guilty from the information I'm directed to gather."

He turned to her, "Jez, a dog won't bite the hand of one that feeds it." She let his words sink in slowly, trying to come up with a counter comment, and held the attitude that this time he was wrong. However, the ensuing months revealed to her he was correct. All of those she listed and supported with evidence of illegal counterfeiting activities were let off the hook. The things she sought to uncover in the fields and cities were happening in the capital. Who could she tell those things to, and who would believe her? Shortly thereafter, she left Washington in disgust.

Later, Baker asked her to investigate a spiritualist group to ensure they weren't unduly influencing the president. She met with Lincoln and determined that he was not only humoring his wife in the effort but also learning about Spiritualism. He was of abolitionist leanings as well as practicing temperance. However, while he was not unfamiliar with Spiritualism, on the other side, he was also leery of whether or not it was a truth to be followed and was aware of the possibility of humans using their own beliefs to filter their readings. Nonetheless, he was fascinated. Jezereal was equally fascinated; however, others feared talking with the spirits and what the conversations could portend. She had to talk to Sumersmith about Spiritualism. She didn't know anything about it.

"So, are you the least bit afraid of making contact with the dead?"

"Oh, I don't know if that's what really happening. I can't say I would be. I learned a long time ago from my momma that it's not the dead to be afraid of. It's the breathing and the supposed 'thinking kind' that if I'm to be afraid, it's of them. Still, I don't want to be bothered by any of them here or on the other side."

"I wouldn't fool with that stuff if I were you, Jez. Just check it out. Plus, by the way...aren't you the least bit worried? Additionally," Sumersmith interjected, "that they're going to figure out some things about you that, let's say, should remain your business. It could be kind of ugly if it were to be blurted out by the spirits amid mixed company."

Jez said nonchalantly, "I just figure if the communications are real, and if I'm to be pointed out, then it's the will of the spirits for that to occur. I might have to battle my way out of there, but I'll deal with that when it happens. Otherwise, I suppose I'll find out for sure that it's real now, won't I? That would certainly be evidence to believe." Jez nodded while talking, shaking her head simultaneously till it was more or less going in a circle.

Sumersmith wound out the evening with, "True, I suppose. Good luck to you on that. I want to hear all about it, but I don't want to talk about it anymore this evening. I won't be able to sleep."

Jezereal was instructed to meet with James Carver, a more seasoned agent by Baker, to explore ways to find out what was going on with the spiritualist movement and what was to be surmised from their activities. So, she was given a list of participants who engaged in Spiritualist practices associated with Mrs. Lincoln and, by extension, Mr. Lincoln. She first had to figure out what a spiritualist movement was, and therefore, she went to the newspapers of Sumersmith's and then started following the people who were part of the group. She stood secretly outside of the meetings and listened. She ascertained that while their words and beliefs, like talking to the dead, may not have any particular vicissitude, the rhetoric was very similar to the goals of the Union. "Do no harm if you can help it because you will have to deal with it when you're dead, and you can still make amends in this life with those you have harmed if you can communicate with them."

She left one of the meetings as they were closing for the night and thought, "The Lincolns, I can understand their involvement. They've lost children. Wouldn't you want to know your babies are OK? Wouldn't you go into the bowels of hell to find your babies if you had a way? They can see or maybe just feel how all these things are hitting simultaneously. Maybe they are worried about all the changes and just trying to find how to pull it together. I never knew anything about riding a train.

I'd never read a paper like Sumersmith reads them. I know how horrific slavery is; they even killed one of themselves.

What was his name? Oh, John Brown and I really had to dance to get out of looking into Miss Tubman's activities because I could see no wrong. Oh, no. These are things we don't know how to bring all together. Severed hands, horrific, bloodied, lifeless bodies of somebody's child, husband, or brother that they won't ever see here again? Life here is too messed up, and I do not see how this will all come out. I wish I could believe more in God than I do, and maybe I'll have to pay for that on the other side. You only got two choices: 1) praise him or 2) burn in hell. I kind of like a third alternative. I do kind of want to know where my mommas are and if they're OK." She wrote out her report to Mr. Carver to give to Mr. Baker. It stated in conclusion that their practices did not seem to pose a danger to the Union. She never received a positive or negative response.

Spying in Virginia as a Confederate

Jez, dressed in women's clothing, was returning to Union lines while on yet another reconnaissance mission for the Union when she walked right into a group of Confederates. She was told to stand down. A tall white man, about 6'2", approached her. "Stop, or I'll shoot!" Jez was taken off guard. There was no campfire, no one sleeping in an opening, just this man standing in front of her. She screamed, and the man walked up to her, grabbed and smelled her. "Woman! What in the hell are you doing out here at this time of night?" Jez stuttered, "I'm sorry, Sir, taking food to my brother at the camp. I think I'm lost." "Hmm. I don't believe you. You're not going anywhere until the morning. Get down on your knees."

~~~~
~~~~

The following day, as the sun rose, she awakened. Evidently, she'd fallen to the ground in sleep. As she awakened, she found the man staring at her. "Open your eyes. I am Lieutenant Strangfeld. Strangfeld stood and paced in front of her. To Jez, she had the sense that he was suffering from clear madness. As Jezereal sat and listened to Strangfeld, he recounted his many encounters with the enemy. He told her tales of how one could identify the enemy. According to him, the "blue" bastards were as true to their name, lifeless entities, and pale from withdrawal from the God-given sun. She wondered how he could stand by that assertion and make an estimation based on that, as it was summertime, and every face she looked at was darkened and ruddy by the sun. What did he see that she couldn't?

Further, as he continued to assess how to recognize the enemy, he pulled the corner of his glove down to scratch at his wrist. It was as sheer white and void of any sun as the persons he described. He was clothed from the neck down with several layers of uniform. His head was covered in a wider-brimmed hat than the usual officer, which left him fairer in complexion than his comrades with caps that covered their scalps with a shorter brim. She stifled a "whew, Jesus!"

He continued in his excitement of telling a youngling in war how to recognize the enemy. At each revelation of his, she became proceedingly quieter, with no need for "really?" or expressions of amazement for his benefit. But, he took her quietness for awe of his knowledge and experience. When he told her that he had been "ordained by God to kill as many enemies to the cause of the secessionists, even she or he'd kill himself if he thought it would advance the cause, or found himself wanting. She, outside herself, drew a breath at the admonition. Strangfeld was duly pleased with that. She'd recognized his ordination and gift to glory. He sat back. Both were quiet. Jezereal was lost in the throes of how deeply committed this man was and how she was going to get as far away from him as she could, or what that all might mean if she couldn't. She looked at him in silence and dubbed him "Lt. Strange." He took her silence as a moment to reflect on her own, or in his mind as "his" own commitment to the cause. He reared back, opened the collar of his shirt, unbuttoned the first two buttons, reached into his chest, and pulled out a leather thread upon which clanked upon his breast a necklace. Jezereal focused on the brown leathery baubles hanging from the leather, and she drew another breath...of terror. They were severed ears.

Jezereal pulled her knife from her boot to kill him on the spot, but a man announcing himself as Private Jones stepped into the clearing. "Lieutenant, your presence is requested..." Strange quickly deposited the ears to his chest and turned to Jones to hear the request. Jezereal was immediately forgotten. After Strange left, Jezereal remained in front of their fire. Jez had to make sense of what had transpired, what almost had happened, and the potential outcome had she killed him. What could be done, knowing what she knew about this man and wondering how many of them were like him? Jezereal thought about the men whose ears hung around Strangfeld's neck.

She sat until well after the timbers had died and until the cold awakened her bones to the need for movement. Strangfeld was something different, something she'd never seen before or ever could believe existed. "Was it all that serious, all that evil? To take a man's ear, men's ears, and wear it at your breast? What consolation, honor, could it possibly give? Is the war this horrific?" Jezereal thought. "Where did it cross the line for him, any of us?"

After the timbers burned to ash and nothing but the sky witnessed her there, she felt hot. Her body felt so hot to her that she felt sickened and nauseated. She couldn't breathe. Her breast bindings were too tight; her head felt too tight in its cap with thoughts and beliefs about what she was doing. She wanted to rip off everything. She couldn't remove anything, though.

There was nowhere to go. She had to just sit there emotionally and mentally bound. Jez had to find a place to lie down within the parameters of the company or out on the edges until she could make it back, with the discomfort in her soul.

Nine

JEZEREAL IN THE WOODS

Jezereal spent the night walking through a sparsely wooded area. She didn't light a lamp; she tried to make her way by moonlight. The going was slow, but she knew the area at least by day and hadn't detected any particular need for caution. Snakes were always a problem but not a particular concern. It was still too cold for copperheads to bother anyone, and it was about the only venomous one in the area. If it were summer, she'd have to take precautions against it. But, at the moment, she was more leery of the two-legged ones. It wasn't the first time, and surely it would not be the last time she'd sleep beneath the clear cover of the night.

Traveling undercover, although a dangerous affair for a woman at any time, was now highly apparent to her that it was especially so in times of war or other civil unrest. "We're all losing our minds to some degree," she thought. "How long can I continue to deal with their insanity and not lose my mind? Today, I'm not especially worried or afraid. I've seen the face of evil so often that maybe I'm just getting hard and don't fear it. It is as it is, an entity to be dealt with." She thought to herself,

"Yeah, right, keep talking to yourself." She whispered under her breath.

It was a beautiful morning, even if a bit crisp, and there was the hanging scent of gunpowder in the air. Jezereal recognized what that meant, and she skirted the edges of a battlefield. Bodies of the fallen were being loaded onto ambulances to be carried back to town. It would take days to complete the cleanup of the carnage. Her only thought was to get to Lederberg to sleep for the night. She considered asking for a ride on one of the ambulances but didn't feel the need for conversation; she preferred no conversation. She just had had enough of talking or being in the presence of others for a while. There had been too many words, and all the words had led to this and countless others she had been to before. All she could hear and couldn't really stand to hear was the deafening silence of the dead. And, at that moment, if she never talked to another living soul again for a long time, that would be too soon.

She had about twenty miles to go on foot and was worn. The battle that had produced the diabolical scene had not been one she'd been involved in, but she knew it now all too well. So, she just wanted to get around it, beyond it.

There was movement in the bushes about twenty yards ahead of her path in an overgrown bush not blighted by the former fray. Jezereal slowed her steps, drew her pistol, and pointed it toward the bush. "Come out of there!" She waited. "Come out, or I'll fill that bush with all kinds of lead. You hear me!" The bush lifted, and a brown, scraggly dog ambled out carrying something black in its mouth. Its head was bowed and it simply approached in her direction as if it were used to coming on command. She relaxed her grip on the gun and allowed her arm to drop to her side. "Whatcha got there, boy?" She took a long look as the dog crossed toward her and could see tits hanging. "Uh, girl, what ya got? "Stop!" she commanded, and the she-dog did as told. Jezereal leaned forward to better see what the dog had in her mouth. "Drop it!" The dog did again as told. She leaned forward, and the dog dropped a severed human hand on the ground before her. "Lord Jesus! Shit, dog!" She screamed so loud and swung her rifle off her shoulder to shoot the dog, the hand. She didn't really know which, but she stopped herself.

"Damn, dog! What do you got? A hand in your mouth!" She stifled a scream and backed up. Then she stepped forward to see if it really was a hand and stepped back, assured that it was a hand. Then, on instinct, she swung the butt of her rifle and batted the hand into a nearby clearing. The dog whimpered and cringed from her scream but was equally torn between running from her and toward the hand. The dog's fear failed her, and she cringed while still heading in the direction of the hand. "No!" Jezereal hollered again, and the dog stopped, squatted, and trembled. "Oh, Christ." Jezereal recognized starvation in the dog.

She'd seen it wrapping itself over the bodies of soldiers marching lean and gaunt on dirty, disheveled, slow-moving women and languid, squalid children. The children had worried her heart to no end. Earlier on in that year of the war, she'd been able to convince some in her company to share a bit of their rations with the children they found along the way. But as the war year wore on, everyone's rations became further and fewer between. It became an anguish to care for the self, and they'd have to turn their heads away as they passed. She knew it was a sin to leave the little ones to starve, but after a night of giving away her last rations to a mother and two children, she'd felt the raw pains of hunger so deep that she'd even put dirt in her mouth just to feel there was something there. She spitted it out, remembering one little family of whites she happened upon in the woods near Wooten, SC.

The children barely moved from their front steps when she approached. A tiny ten-year-old boy had risen to call out to his momma that a man was approaching. Momma came out wary but obviously harmless. She attempted the pleasantries and absently primped, pulling the loose strands of her hair that hadn't been washed in a long time behind her ear and smoothing a dusty white shift with a frayed hem. They both realized at the same time that the dress was ripped below her left breast, and she modestly tried to pull it closed. She couldn't keep her eyes on Jezereal's face. Her gaze drifted from Jez's face and hung on the knapsack hanging from Jez's shoulder.

Jezereal glanced down at her knapsack and then at the little children who had quietly moved toward them until they were sitting on the porch at Jezereal's feet, their eyes, too, reaching into the sack. Jezereal weighed the situation. She was going to have to feed, not understanding of their condition.

Loved and cherished animals forsaken by stewards caught up in their own terrors, left to live or die by their own devices after years of pampering and service. And here was one of the discarded lying in front of her, ready to feed on a human hand. Jezereal considered the import of the scene she had witnessed before her. "Was it the hand of her master that she has carried in love or for comfort, or maybe it was hunger driving her to feed on it?"

It hadn't actually bitten into it from what she could remember seeing. It looked like a clean sever, albeit a bit of a hack job, than if it had been chewed off. Maybe a field surgeon had done some poor devil that particular service. She mused, "The spoils of war go to the victor. Who is to say who the victor will be in this battle? Perhaps in the end, we'll all destroy ourselves; the victors will be life itself, the earth, and the least of us. In the scheme of things, maybe that's something to hope for. Humans (and somewhere, there was an inkling that this included her as well) have made these people.

She asked the woman if she had a place where she could sleep for the night, and the woman nodded without removing her eyes from the bag. I have some food I can pay you with, and the woman fainted into Jezereal's arms, and the babies began crying. Jezereal picked her up, carried her into the house, and laid her on a ragged bed. It was a desolate little place. The children, rickety and unsure of step, followed them into the house. Jez asked the oldest boy where she could get water, and the boy told her that the pond was down the way and pointed. She didn't have much to feed them, but she drew a bucket of water from the pond that appeared muddy and possibly tainted. Jez returned to the house, made a fire, and boiled the water. She poured the top off the water and, in another pail, boiled it again until she finally got clear water.

Jezereal threw the dirty water out, and when she came back in, the oldest boy was in her knapsack feasting. She snatched the food from his mouth and told him she was sorry, but he'd have to wait until it was finished so they'd all have enough. She would have to boil the Johnny cakes down into a slurry soup, so they all would have enough of something in their stomachs.

She asked the boy what they'd been eating, and he said, "Momma's been making us cookies." That struck Jez as unusual; considering the lack, she saw nothing close to food. But, the boy pointed to a bucket of clearly rancid tallow, then he pointed to a half bag of salt, and then to a bowl of dirt. "That's what momma uses to make the cookies." Dirt cakes. They'd been eating dirt cakes.

Remembering that family, Jez shook her head while look-ing at the dog. Animals didn't look or act too differently than humans. Everywhere in everything, there was evidence of an annihilation of life. The trees and shrubs didn't evidence any anger with their plight...unnatural wounds, lame, and cut down in their life cycle, the dead and the dying. Wild beings' sensi-bilities were discombobulated, leaving their young, eating their young, attacking their own, their only consolation being un-awareness and ugly mess of it all, slavery, war, hunger...people eating pure dirt to survive, blood brother killing brother in hide-ous ways, women fighting war brought on by men, and children who will pay witness and homage to it all only for their futures to be destroyed as well. The fathers' sins were perpetrated and perpetuated through the lives of the children. Maybe it is best to just let the animals reap the bounty of the dead and for life to move on. Maybe the Garden will be again what it once was before we came along and made an abomination of it all." She walked on and left the dog where it was.

On one occasion, Jez heard a dog whimpering when she fired at a bird for dinner. She was curious because she hadn't seen any dogs since the one she saw with the hand. Jezereal sat quietly on a stump and listened and watched. Shortly, she heard a rustling in the trees near her, and she readied her gun, thinking it might be dinner after all. It was the dog from the field. Even though she didn't talk to him, the dog continued to follow her as she headed back to camp. As time passed, she finally allowed her-self to talk to the dog, and the canine became her companion. They walked together, and Jez began to notice that not only was the dog reacting strangely skittish for a dog, but other animals seemed just as skittish to her. Jez remembered talking to a man who told her they'd been trying dog hides for leather in Georgia. Jezereal was appalled and began contemplating yet another way the animals were affected. She promised herself if they made it out alive, she'd find her a home without the noise that had become frighteningly evident, everything that breathed.

Tired of the endless thoughts, Jez thought of her times and how things hadn't changed much for children and the ongoing issues of poverty. Men separated from women and social norms that looked only to get far worse than better as time progressed. The dysfunction of family life due to the world's greed. The powers that be and their Wars.

Jezereal felt body aches as she felt the warmth of the fire, unlike many with age. Her joints did not ache due to age, but the relentless actions of her youth had finally caught up with her. A few areas of concern, old war wounds made themselves known. However, thinking of many who did not work as hard as they fared worse due to non-active lifestyles. She stretched, reached over to finish her second cup of tea, and looked at the bottom of the now-empty cup. Thinking of refilling, she paused, then pushed again with her feet, and the chair rocked her back into slumber, and she dreamed about her past life... letting go of the thought of tea.

Johnny Cake Boys

"What in the world is wrong with you, happy fellows? What's so funny?" Jez asked as she wandered toward a group of men in Union garb. She wouldn't have approached them, but her horse had gone lame, and she was on foot again. She could have slept alone, but there was something about them, maybe the fire and their camaradcric, that drew her to them. The evening fire illuminated three men rolling on the ground, howling and laughing. There were five altogether. They were shocked when she slipped into their midst as they were intent on merriment. Jez introduced herself as Jessie White on her way to see her sister, but her horse had gone lame, and she was walking the rest of the way to get help for her horse. They promised Jez that they could help her see to it in the morning. They welcomed her into their midst and expressed how unfortunate it was for her to experience a lamed horse. They introduced themselves: Timothy, Loren, Jonathan, Rory, and Lt. Cargill. She settled down in front of a fire amongst them.

Jonathan, a private, pointed to Timothy. "Miss Jessie, you see, you...see, that fool there? He cooked us up some plaster of fucking Paris for dinner. Oh, excuse me, Miss. Didn't mean to curse in front of you." "It's quite OK. I've heard far worse, and I came into your camp. You sound like my brother." If you're sure...you're sure, Miss? OK, thought it was flour for the Johnny cakes, but it was fucking Plaster of Paris. Hard as a rock." Jonathan, trying to catch his breath before another pending outbreak of laughter, managed to say, "And then Loren tried to bite it. Broke his fucking tooth. Should have known better than to bite down on that. It wouldn't even brown, but he was so damn hungry! It was worse than eatin' hardtack. Don't nobody just bite down on Hardtack, but Johnny cake...? More laughter erupted from the guys. "Didn't expect that, did ya? You are now one toothless bastard. Timothy, that'll teach you to "harvest" flour from a blown-up train. Taste it first, will ya?" And they were off laughing again from the ridiculousness of trying to eat a plaster of Paris Johnny Cake.

Timothy choked out, "Fuck you. It was white. It looked like flour, didn't it? Didn't nobody else think anything different, did you?" Jonathan and Loren both jumped at that. "Cause you said, 'Look, I done found some flour!'" "We took your word for it. You're the fucking cook." Timothy sat back upon a log and looked long into the fire. "It was heavy tho...for flour." They all broke out again into raucous laughter. Jezereal loved the sound of pure merriment, which is why she loved to hear children laugh. There was spirituality in laughter that always touched her deeply. It was the laughter enjoyed by all at no one in particular's expense. Because each person involved in the moment could see the ridiculousness of the situation. These were the moments Jezzie could allow herself to feel humanly connected to others, with no harm intended to anyone. She laughed, and them, seeing her laugh for the first time, touched them and tempered their laughter in a sweet way.

They wanted to hear more of her, a woman laugh, so they kept on egging each other, elaborating on the story, until tears streamed from her eyes, and she begged them to stop. Jonathan kept going, "And, then Loren is yelling at Timothy to hurry up, forget browning the shit. He is hungry now!" "Please, you're all a bunch of damn fools, stop, quit; I can't take anymore." She held the back of her head; the bones at the base of her skull were straining with the unaccustomed feel of such intense laughter.

As the laughter subsided, Loren said, "Shoot, I'm still hungry though. If I swallow a piece of this, do you think it'll kill me? I mean, it ain't like I ain't eaten dirt before. Shit, one time I dreamed about eatin' dirt. It was so good, soft, sweet, and at the same time tastin' like I was eatin' meat. It was the best thing I could dream of eatin'. So, the next morning, I rolled over and was so excited 'cause there was a lot of it around, and I swept up some dirt in my mouth and ate it. My stomach cramped like shit an hour later, but I couldn't tell if it was from the dirt or if I was still hungry for more! But, it didn't matter either way though 'cause wasn't nothin' else comin'." The boys had stopped laughing. Evidently, they all knew the taste of dirt, and it had been good at some point.

Jezereal pulled her pack from around her shoulders, opened it, and offered hard tack and dried beef. She had enough to last her a week, but it amounted to a sumptuous meal for a night between the four of them. A woman could find food readily the next day if she were smart enough and willing to sashay into the midst of possible dangerous men and situations. Still, only Providence knew when and what the men would have to eat or meet.

They thanked her in such gratuitous words and dove into the food she offered. When all was consumed, although not full, they were relieved to have something on their stomachs besides the taste of Paris plaster. As they each found a comfortable space to call it a night, their conversation turned from their stomachs to their lives. Loren lay back on his knapsack and said, "You know, I'll be glad when this shit is over. When I'm back home with my wife and kids. I wasn't expecting to be gone from them this long. I was just going to come out here because I figured I could make some money to feed them and maybe make it a little better when I got back home. Just never figured I'd have to keep doing this for so long. It's hard for my family back home, and as long as I stay in it, it's a little better for them...that is, if I don't get killed. I'm not sure what will happen to them if I don't make it, but I have to do it for now. But, as soon as it's over, I'll be back with them.

Timothy quipped, "You got a wife? Who would want you? Let you between her legs? Produce children? Somethings wrong with that!" Loren raised an eyebrow and said, "Keep talking, and something will be wrong with you." Everyone laughed.

"Ok, really, all foolin' aside, it's nice you got a family. I don't have anything to go back home to, nothing I want anymore. I'm my own man out here. Just gotta do what all them above me tell me to do, but that ain't nothin'. Done worse in life. My daddy... Anyway, I ain't never been further than my town, and at least now I've been someplace. When this is over, for me, I think I'm travelin' out West. I've met people who tell me to go to California or Nevada. Hell, why not go see what's out there. It sure beats the hell out of here and where I come from.

Rory, a minister's son, said, "I've heard tell of what you were saying earlier. Lieutenant, about negros, fighting on both sides, but I have not yet seen it for myself. Even if there are some Negros fighting for the Confederacy, I suppose that's understandable. If you've been trained like an animal to do as you're told, I suppose you would, even unto death. Perhaps some of them have no desire to be free as they would lose their way of the only life they've ever known: food and shelter. My father was poor when we fought for our freedom against the Brits, and he told me black men fought alongside him then for the independence we worship now. So, I don't know. I would like to meet one of them, I guess. Not now, of course, but I would at some point, just to make sense of it."

"Well, I came to fight because it's the right thing to do. My daddy is a preacher, and he doesn't believe people should be slaves like the Hebrews were in the good book. I heard that all my life from him, and by God, if he could have left his flock to come to fight himself, he would have, but my brother and I couldn't let Daddy even think about leaving Momma, the kids, and the church. So, we're here. Free the slaves. We free the Union to be what it's supposed to be in God's eyes.

I can't say nothing 'gainst no body's daddy, 'specially not no preacher. Even with all my ways yall can witness, stand up in the church and damn me to hell for, I'm God fearin' if the truth be told, and right now ain't no time to lie 'bout nothing. We could be bloatin up in the sun tomorrow. But I'm tellin' you preacher's son and all that's none of our business what they do with slaves down here. It's just what they do; truth be known, they got slaves up North, too. As far as I can see, they just call them servants but don't treat 'em too much better. Its people with money treat us all the same, po white folks, bad as the niggras. But, shoot, I aint fightin for no black folks because I have to help my damn self. If you try to tell me that's what I could get kilt for, to save some darkies' asses from the plow, I'd get right up and walk away from this shit right now. That ain't what this is 'bout fo' me. Plus, damn, I seen some nigga rebel once, or rather I don't know what I seent cause I was so shocked I almost got myself kilt looking at him before someone else shot his ass. Didn't have time to really go back and look, but that shit made my damn head itch. What the hell you and yo daddy fightin' for when they don't really want it and would shoot the shit out of a Federal to protect they mastah? So, figure don't make no sense to fight for somebody that don't need to be fought for. Spit on that. I just wan' to get through this alive, take my pension, and get on wit' my life.

Jezereal lay quietly, feigning sleepiness. It was certainly an argument she'd heard in various circles throughout the North and the South. She roused herself and said: "We all stupid in one way or another on this!" She shook her blanket out and onto the ground. "Why you say it like that?" Lt. Cargill had sipped out of his bottle of whiskey throughout the evening and was now fairly "tight." She immediately sensed she'd gone too far, even though the others were laughing at her, calling them stupid in some way.

Their mood and merriment hadn't changed, but Cargill's had. Lt. Cargill had never offered any words or laughter in the brief time she'd known him. He sat off the side of the main group. She wondered what had made him a Lieutenant, what those who'd made him Lt. had seen in him. But with his question, she'd instantly reconsidered. He had enough sense to question her, and she didn't sense drunken malice, but a keen and direct question that went beyond plaster Johnny cakes.

"Oh, I didn't mean nothing! Just silly, funny." "No, maybe you didn't say it, but you meant something' else." "Maybe you heard something else, but I wasn't saying anything." "Come on, don't shit me. I've seen how you look at them. I know how you think about people. You sit and watch, but you don't say nothing. Now you call us all stupid. What you saying? I want to know how stupid we are to you."

Jez wouldn't be pushed this evening. It was late; he was drunk. Hell, she was sleepy and wasn't ready for a fight on any level. She looked him straight in the eye and said, "Let it rest. It'll be morning soon enough. Talk to me then if you still have a mind to." Jonathan and Loren began chiding Cargill to shut up and let everyone sleep. They'd already flopped down and covered up. It'd been fun, and no one was ready to stoke any fires for the evening. The times just were forcing them to do things they wouldn't have typically done or even conceived they'd do. As she tried to drift off to sleep, Jezereal knew they fought for many reasons. She understood from working through both lines that there were many good men and women at heart.

As she drifted to sleep, she considered her past weeks living in the outdoors. She was outside, blanket on the ground, no tent to cover, mosquitoes whizzing past her ears until she pulled the blanket over her head, three men, full, exhausted from the day's skirmish, snoring loudly nearby. Jez was happy...happier than she had felt, and in a time longer than her memory could recall. She looked at the plaster johnnycake curing on the fire's edge; she smiled and yet felt a bit sad as she drifted into slumber, "Not much is as it seems anymore." Listening to the men, she, as she went into sleep, heard herself say, "You're going back."

Ten

JEZEREAL'S ENCOUNTER WITH A SLAVE WHO IS A SLAVE HUNTER

Jezereal looked out her window after she arrived at the fort the following day and said goodbye to her companions. Stories of her past flowed like water from a stream within her mind as she turned from the window and looked at herself in a mirror. Jez smiled ever so slightly as she thought of the many people she had met who concealed their true identity, as she had physically, mentally, and emotionally. One thing was true: people ran toward or away from their reality, but always thinking of better life paths that would be construed or misconstrued as for the good or for ill in the future.

Looking in the mirror, Jez asked herself, *What does one consider when they want a better life?* She remembered an incident as she looked at herself in the mirror and thought of Clem. *That was one crazy fool.* Jezereal saw herself in a shallow tree, having been run up on by a pack of dogs. She had been scurrying again through the night when she heard the barking. She realized they were coming rapidly in her direction. She couldn't outrun the dogs at the pace they were setting, so she swiftly climbed the tree.

Shortly after the dogs rounded her loft of branches and leaves, a black man with a lantern stepped beneath the tree. "Hey, you, come down here! Come on now, you can't stay there all night, and if you don't come down, I'll come up there!"

Jez shouted, "Leave me be. I have a gun and will shoot you."

"Well, now you could shoot me, but you still wouldn't get down without my dogs eating you alive." He put out the light from his lantern. "Now, hit me and my dogs! He cackled. Jez knew there was naught to do but sit in the tree until morning. The following day, he and his dogs were still there.

"Oh, well," she thought and climbed down. The man called off his dogs. She alighted, and he approached her with his dogs yapping and surrounding her. He grabbed her, and his eyes intensified on her face.

"Wha chu tryin' to do gal? Yo sho enuf white nuf to pass. That's for damn sho, but I'm wha chu'd call an expert in bloodlines. I runs the massa's dogs, and I kin tell the blood in humans, can smell it damn neah as well as I kin tell the blood in dogs. And, you got some darkie blood for sho. I can smell it!"

"You're crazy! You let me go. I'm a white woman, and I won't stand for how you're treating me. Let me go now, or so help me, they'll hang you for what you're doing!"

"Don't try to throw me off yo scent gal wit yo fine werds. I kin smell wha yo et lass night! Comin' all off ya. Nigga food, gal, nigga food. White fokes got a differen smell from wha dey eats. That ain't it doe, niggas got something in their bodies that just make em smell differen' from white folks, an slant eye folks, an injuns..huh?

"Line em up and make em run, and I can tell you which one wen whicha way. Yo close doh, real close. But, naw, yo ain't no white gal. Got me a nigga play actin white." He howled with laughter, skipped around her like he'd discovered a great treasure, and couldn't wait to tell his master.

"You runs dogs, huh? After what, niggas?" Jezereal eyed the black man warily. She showed no fear; she could feel that he was sniffing her out, so to speak, testing her. He might be a threat; she wasn't sure yet. Jez wondered if she would have to kill him and if she could do that without killing a dog cause, surely he'd call the dogs on her if they were in a fight.

"Coons, fox...niggas on occasion," the latter words came slyly if not matter-of-factly. No shame or dis-consternation with what he had to do when he had to do it.

"Um, hum, let's see, you, me, no matter what you think I am, dogs, coons, foxes, rats, we all the same to you, huh? Wild, enslaved, free, white? All animals still to you, huh? The black man shrugged.

"Nah, girl, weez not that much differen' far as I can see in this 'hol thin' here." On a nearby tree stump, he eased himself down, delighted with his catch for the day.

Jezereal felt anger, disgust, and fear rising in her. The fear was unsettling to her, and she had to wonder because there wasn't anything in her, a cause of...you do this to me...and an effect...I'll do this to you.

She hadn't done anything to him yet but just be there. She understood people did things to each other out of their own quiet hell, invisible to others. Thus, she couldn't say anything. She just hadn't dealt with a black man, or any man, so dead to his own situation. There had been house slaves fighting for their own place in the hierarchy of the slave household, but they didn't have any great love for white folks. They were just making it the best way they could through life. And, she'd met tricksters who were out for their own and they didn't give a shit about whites or blacks or anyone else but themselves.

She'd known blacks full of fear of pain and death who did what they did to protect themselves and their loved ones. She'd known and felt deeply for those who fought to show that they were 'people' good human beings who just wanted to prove they were patriots for righteousness. Some saw righteousness in States' rights, and some saw righteousness as she did in the Union. She could understand all those black folks, but she had never met a black man who saw himself as an animal and as the harbinger of death for any of his own kind, animal or human, based on who was the most likely to survive. And, in this war, who knew how the wind would blow? But even that didn't seem to be a concern. He'd just hunt. He could and would maim and or kill anything, and that was not a man she'd ever reckoned with before.

Being that she was in captivity of a deadly opponent, Jezereal decided, *What the hell, do not show fear,* so she amped down her feelings of fear and let out a sigh of resignation to his will. Then, she asked the question as if seeking his advice.

"What would you have me as? A slave to some nasty God-forsaken white man? Someone who could use me any old kind of way? I was done so many ways wrong in my life before you even knew you were a nigga and a slave. You be some kind of true crazy to think I'd not use to or I'd do what I could to get out of that. Does your master treat you as well as you treat Puddin?"

The man sat back and then lunged at Jez. "You, bitch, Puddins' a good a dog! I'll cut yo fuckin' thoat if you got anythin' bad to say bout her!" In his lunge, he landed on top of her and held his knife just under Jez's nose. While he was screaming at her, Jez thought, *Shit, he's going to cut off my nose. Well, I can live without my nose. Calm down and talk to this nigga, get him off my nose, and maybe I can get him off me. What did I say? What did I say about fucking Puddin?"*

He was breathing heavily, and his body weight had her pinned. She relaxed, letting her natural inclinations to fight him drain. When the fight within her was removed, she simply looked long into his eyes and said, "Nigga, what is wrong witch you? I didn't say nothin' gainst Puddin'. I don't know nothing 'bout Puddin', but I gotta figure she's bitch of the bitches. Shit, she tree'd my ass. Shit, the bitch is bettern' than any bitch I've ever seen. Get yo ass off me. I wann't sayin' nothing bad 'bout her!

The man eased his grip on the back of her neck and lowered the knife from her nose, but not quite far enough from her neck. She still had some talking to do. "Puddin' is smart. I KNOW that. And, she's a pretty d...," Jezereal figured she'd better not call her a dog... "she's pretty and playful when she's with you. She's good with her pups, and she's alert. She's just a...she's just beautiful." The man slowly pulled away from her, stepped back to his stump, and sheathed his knife into his pocket. "Ya know. I got Puddin' when she was just a pup, and her momma didn't want her, tried to damn near eat her. But, I got er 'way from er, and I fed er. Puddin' slep wif me all her life. I couldn't luv nothin' like I luv Puddin.

Jezereal studied this man because now she realized he knew something about love. He couldn't connect with a human or most other animals, but he could connect with this one dog.

"Massa don't treat me bad like most white folks treats they niggas. He's beat me. He feeds me pretty well, though. I can get a pass when I needs to get something for me or the dogs. And, I gets to keep the dogs and hunt with them."

"That's a fine life, I guess, if you can keep it, and it's good that you've had a good master. I just don't want to be owned by anyone ever again."

What you thin' bout dis her Massa Lincoln? Yo thin, really, he give a shit about yo, me any nigga's, po ass white people?

He don'. I know how yo think of me. I tell you this. Yo is the crazy one."

Jez had to think about that. She'd met "Massa Lincoln," and truth be told, she wasn't sure what to think of him, what he would do or be in the end for the country, for her, for the po white folk. She'd "sniffed" him out, too, and wasn't quite sure where his allegiances would finally run. He was playing party politics, and the stakes were grave. But, he said, in the end, slaves were merely resources for the war effort to supply the Union, and if the Union failed, what then?

She'd never truly considered that the Union could fail until that moment, even after all she'd seen and been through. But, now, sitting with a man totally out of his mind as a human being, as mad as others she'd seen, but his thoughts were different. Everyone was driven stone crazy by the conditions that prevailed. Jezereal found herself pinned down again, mentally and emotionally; bullets were flying at her from all directions. There was nothing she could do at the moment. She was exhausted, and her mind was whirling out of control. She rolled over, turning her back on the man. He was going to do what he would. She couldn't loosen her bounds, and she was pretty sure he wasn't going to kill her, so Jez just went to sleep.

Clem's master had been alerted by a hunter that Clem was holding a woman captive, and he went out to find him. It was midnight. Clem had started moving in the night, rising to his knees. Jez also moved right behind him. He was breathing deeply of the air. The dogs were moving, sniffing, and alert to movements coming toward them. They weren't sensing a stranger; it was Master Jim approaching. Clem ordered her beneath the bed. When she was under, he pulled the blanket down to cover the side. Clem stepped outside. Jezereal heard him hail his master. "Massa Jim, why yo her dis late?"

She waited. Jim must have pushed past Clem because she heard the door thrown back and boots on the floor. The room was black. "Why am I out here? I got to have a reason? You ain't never asked me why I do anythin' I do. Why you ask me? "Clem went silent. Jezereal knew he was tensing. She could hear the anxiety in the dogs. Clem had left the door open and the dogs were milling anxiously about the doorway. "What you got goin on down here?"

"Nothin goin heya, suh. I wuz sleep. Da dogs woke me, tellin me ya wuz comin'." "Uh, huh, the dogs woke ya."

"Yeh, suh." Jim walked around the room in the dark. "Well, I'm here! Light a fucking candle! Yo Massa is here!" "Yes, suh. Lemme see if I got some candle or somethin'." He went to the table where he'd put the candle out only minutes before. "Suh, I ain ga nothing to light it wi. Let's go ouside.

Mo light ou der dan in heya." "Na' I wanna be in here." Jim pulled out a match and struck it on the sole of his boot. "Now, we got some light. Shit, Clem, there's a candle." He lit the candle, and there was light in the room. He turned to Clem. "You been kind of cagey for the last couple of days. Somethin' ain't right with you down here. Whatcha hidin' Clem?" Jim looked around the room, turning his back on the bed; Massa Jim faced Clem. Jezereal knew he knew she was beneath it, but she made no move.

<div align="center">~~~~</div>

Daylight streamed through the window and illuminated the room. When Clem came to, something was lying heavily on top of him, and he found his breathing labored. Slowly coming to his senses, he groaned and pushed the weight off of him. Clem sat up and rubbed the back of his head and felt an angry knot. He shook his head to clear it and rubbed his forehead. Another equally hot but arced welt ran from his forehead to his cheek. What had happened? He couldn't quite remember. Why was he on the floor? He went to put one hand down to push himself up off the floor, and instead of feeling a solid floor, he was pushing into something much softer. He realized that was the weight that had been on top of him. He pulled himself to his knees for a better look. It was Massa Jim. Clem put his hand over Jim's nose, felt nothing, and lowered his face to Jim's. He couldn't feel any warmth or air emitting from his nose or mouth. Jim wasn't breathing. Clem sat back on his haunches and wondered how long he had been dead, and he wasn't quite sure why he had awakened to Jim being on top of him.

Jumping up and looking around the room, Clem noticed, Jez was gone. Not like he'd expected her to be there. Looking back down at Jim, Clem ran out the door to check on his dogs. With Jim lying there like that, it was going to go really bad for him if Jezereal wasn't found soon. Clem didn't know how long he'd been out, but even if a day behind, he could catch her. He and his girls would bring Jez back and turn her in as the killer of Jim, and he'd be free to go his way. *Damn, though,* Clem thought. *I had a good thing and allowed a woman to mess up my life. But, he'd fix it. Fix her, yes, but let the dogs mess her up a little first.* That'd show the white folks, he wasn't kidding about getting Massa Jim's killer.

Clem yelled for Puddin but didn't hear her yelp back, as was her custom when she was called. He stopped and listened but didn't hear any of his babies as he ran to where he'd tied up his number one love. There, she lay sprawled on the ground at the end of her rope with a bullet between her eyes, not moving like Massa Jim. He called her name gently, waiting and searching with his eyes all over her body for some sign of movement or response. "Puddin? Oh, Puddin!" He fell to the ground and cud-dled close to her. He ran his hand over her body, lifted her head, and kissed her all over her face. She was cold and stiff. He'd seen death many times of man and animal, and it had never even been a thought about the pain that one might suffer prior to death. And even though Puddin went quick, he still worried that she might have felt the pain of the bullet hitting her or that she didn't die right away, just laying out there dying alone. His eyes welled with tears as he picked up his love and carried her to their hut. He stepped on and over the body of Massa Jim, and as he laid Puddin gently on his bed, he vowed to her that he'd get Jezereal and kill her in a way worse than she'd killed Puddin.

As much as it hurt Jezereal to kill any animal other than for food, Puddin' and the others had to be put down first of all because they were of a vile nature, albeit not of their own making, but most of all because with them on her scent, she wouldn't stand a chance of getting away. Some slaves she'd met along the way told her that if you made it to a river, you might be able to cross before they could pick her scent up again. However, Jezereal figured that would only work if you were entering free territory; otherwise, the dogs could just pick up your scent again once they got across.

A man she met on his way to prison for committing a murder in a small town and who had been on the run told her, thinking she, rather he, was on the run, too, that onions and mud would do the trick and throw a dog off of one's scent, or cayenne pepper would mess up their noses for a couple of hours. She couldn't confirm any of those methods as accurate, and Clem would not confirm or deny, and, anyway, she didn't have any of those things readily at her disposal at the moment of her escape. No, there was no other choice but to kill them. Clem and those dogs would hunt her for days. As it was, he'd probably try to hunt her for years anyway. She thought to herself, "Should have killed Clem too." But she couldn't because, other than holding her prisoner, he hadn't really hurt her all that much. Mean words and threats, a punch or two over the weeks, he'd held her, but she'd taken way more than that from those in life who actually owned her.

She never really understood why Clem held her. He didn't turn her over to Jim, and he hadn't tried to touch her sexually. She was just there. She wasn't even as useful to him as Puddin. Maybe he just liked to have an almost white-looking woman under his control. It happened quickly after Massa Jim had reeled around from Clem and kicked the bed over, exposing her. Jez had been ready. When the bed flew high, she'd caught the end of it and swung it at Jim. Jezereal clipped him on the side of the head. Clem had snatched his gun and attempted to shoot Jezereal, but she'd feinted to the left and reeled behind Jim. Jim stumbled in the bullet's path, and it hit him square in his right temple. Clem was shocked when he realized he shot Jim and screamed, "Massa!"

As Clem bent to catch him, Jezereal grabbed a skillet off the table and smashed Clem in the back of the head. He was knocked out cold. She'd hit him again as he was falling backward from the weight of Jim. Then she hit him again as he went down.

Outside the door stood a horse. Jezereal deftly mounted and started riding away from the house. It was Jim's horse, and it was a good one. She was surprised at how well he obeyed her commands, so she rode him as hard as possible, not knowing the terrain and skirting the roads. After an hour's ride of slowing, finding a wider space, riding hard, and then slowing again, she saw lights in the distance and rode toward them, but not directly. There might be dogs, slavers, or soldiers; she didn't know what or which, and although worn out with fatigue, she thought she might get close enough to find a place nearby to rest for the night and try to figure out her next move. She could go in as a woman or steal some clothes and go in as a man. She wasn't sure which she would have to do, but Jez didn't have time to think much beyond that when the horse reared up high, and she went airborne.

"Christ!" she screamed as she found herself grabbing at the air and kicking with nothing to hold her in the night sky. She only had enough time to realize she was falling, and all she could think was, "Hope this doesn't kill me." Jezereal hit hard upon the ground. Jezereal was floating in a white space... She'd been there before, it was the same...peaceful and quiet. She was content to be there until she heard the buzzing. It started out small but grew to feel like a hundred flies around both ears. She tried to shake them off of her, and as she did, she realized she couldn't quite get her eyes open. She wanted to see the annoying beasts and what in the world was drawing them to her like that. Even with the buzzing getting louder, she was just as distressed to not be able to open her eyes.

What was wrong with them? Why wouldn't they obey her? They were heavy and didn't respond to her raising her eyebrows to lift them. She tried to lift a hand to smack away the flies, and Catherine O'Ray stood next to Jezereal's bed and watched her attempts at wakening. She and others in their compound had taken turns watching and waiting for these very signs that

Jez's condition was improving; she'd live. Theirs was a secluded space; People never just "happened" by their way.

Catherine thought, "Well, we will have to change that thought to 'rarely.'" This woman landing in their midst was indeed a rarity. They'd been around the fire and heard a horse distressed, followed by a woman's scream and something hitting and smashing what they found to be the wood frame of their composting bin. There she was, sprawled amongst the black, vegetable-enriched soil, with various vegetable elements lying on and around her. She was out cold. No wonder she'd fallen over a cliff 20 feet high. Thankfully, she'd hit the pile a couple of feet the other way, and she might not have had as much life in her as she did, which they worked fervently to keep lit. Her body had been severely jarred, but there were no broken bones that they could find.

Over the next week of her recovery from the fall, Jez attained an understanding of those who were caring for her. They were women that she had heard some whispers about, the Wiccans. Wiccans were women who practiced what they called witch-craft, and when she realized that, she got chills. She was so not sure of what she had "fallen into." What was she to do?

Jezereal knew she couldn't do anything. For a while, she had no idea of what they were about or their intentions concerning her, if any at all. So, she simply just lay there listening. Finally, one day, a few days after her "landing" in their midst, she struggled to set up. Miss. Catherine brought her a bowl of soup and sat down on a seat next to her. She looked at her and said, "Tell me the story. Who were you running so hard from, and why?" Jez told the truth. "It's a black dog runner for his master. He, they, wanted me, but I didn't want them. They'll be coming after me. So, I have to get out of here so they don't hurt any of you." She tried to get up, but Catherine pushed her back down.

She had surmised from her murmuring in her sleep that she was being chased, and the women had talked about what if that was the case. So, they concocted a plan, not really knowing all of the details. They wouldn't let a woman be hurt. And, at that, they put the plan into effect. They devised a scheme that she was to be buried.

They knew the area well and had ways of knowing when Clem or others were coming. They dug a grave in the ground and put cloth all around it. They put in a cord for air for her through the ground and put her in it along with water and jerky. They had given her herbs to put her into a deep sleep. Then, they covered her up with dirt. Clem arrived the next morning at their compound. He was tired and ragged and demanded to see if she was there. He said she was a runaway from his master and had done his master great harm. She was a murderer to be hung. They told him that she had fallen off of a horse and died. They had already buried her, and they pointed to the spot.

Clem demanded to see her body, but they protested; they had just buried her, and she'd only recently died. Clem made them at gunpoint to dig her up, and they did. But, when they opened the coffin, he looked at her from his standing point above the ground and raised his gun to shoot her between her eyes. Catherine threw herself in front of him and shouted at him, "Sir! Before you commit this abomination of the dead, tell us, did she harm you?"

"Yes, she did," Clem said, "She killed a loved one."

Catherine asked, "Did you or your loved one harm her?"

He said, "No, and what does it matter that I put a bullet in the head of a dead woman?"

"Sir! Did you harm her?" He was talking to white people, and he didn't know quite the right way to lie to them all standing around him.

"No, I didn't harm her."

"Sir, then why do you think she would kill your loved one?"

He stumbled in response, "Because she was mean and evil, and she killed Puddin." "Sir, she killed 'Puddin'. Was that the name of your wife?"

"No."

"Your sister?"

"No... yes..."

Catherine said, "I'm so sorry for your loss, Sir, and it doesn't really matter, I guess, but we want to know before if we are to let you commit this abomination upon the dead, the story. Who was Puddin to you?"

Clem realized he was staring into the faces of ten white people. He couldn't figure out what would happen to him if they found out he'd lied, that Puddin wasn't a human, a dog, and what they might tell the others about him committing "an abomination." He didn't know what that word meant, but it meant something bad, considering how they looked at him. So, he uncocked his gun, turned, and walked away. He kept on walking. Clem, no longer the dog runner, knew they had her, dead or alive. Either way, he couldn't effectively kill ten white women to get to one black one. While walking away, Clem understood that he was beaten, and somehow, he gained an admiration for Jezereal. He had to let this "bitch" go. For now, he knew Clem would be the one on the run.

~ Eleven ~

COMING TO TERMS WITH AN OLD GHOST

Jezereal felt nature's call, so she pulled her pot out to relieve herself. As she wiped herself, she observed her legs and thought, *"It was just skin"*.

But humankind had made such a difference between each other's skin color for various reasons, some only known to each person. She recalled Lincoln's speech...March 4, 1861. President Abraham Lincoln stated that he had "no purpose, directly or indirectly, to interfere with the institution of slavery in the states where it exists. I believe I have no lawful right to do so, and I have no inclination to do so." When Jezereal remembered his words and found that little to nothing, if anything, would happen to the counterfeiters, she left Washington in disgust.

As she stood, looking at the skin of her legs, she remembered...and with the memory, felt the old fear and disgust well up within the pit of her stomach. She had not felt that sort of need to vomit in 10 years. It was the source of her dread. A silent belch erupted, and along with it, the smell of death. That same belch had once signaled the urge to extinguish the darkness that stood in opposition to the light that had always dogged each step of her life.

Jez had completed an assignment in Virginia and was on her way home when she received a tip from another agent in another state that there was a plot brewing to assassinate the president in Philadelphia. He asked her to take the case since she was returning to Maryland and would pass through Philadelphia. She could, if she would, investigate it for a few weeks. Somehow, they'd learned Mr. Lincoln would be on his way from his home in Illinois to Washington to be inaugurated in his second term as President. The active parties, or some of them in the business, were understood to be in Philadelphia.

Since Jezereal was not concerned about returning home right away, she sent a telegram stating she would look into it and see what she could find. She telegrammed Baker and Carver using veiled words expressing her concern and whereabouts. As her train pulled into Philadelphia, Jezereal banged her head on the train window when she saw Rory Conyers—the man who killed her mother and used her physically as a child, standing in the square outside the train. Her childhood memories struck like lightning, fast and furious.

The man stood in his barn. It was open-ended. It was sunny outside, and she could see the man standing in the middle of the "livery." He was sharpening tools. She could see sickles and other sharp objects hanging on the walls. He wore high work boots and a heavy black, knee-length apron over his clothing. He was drinking. He'd sharpen a minute and then take a swig of the drink from a bottle half filled with brown liquid. Outside, two boys were peeking into the barn at the man. The boys' figures switched back and forth between rambunctious little boys and then little boys with the heads of differing animals. Jez saw one as a dog, almost a werewolf mask, and the other a warthog with tusks. The little boys were talking. They were maybe 9 and 10 years old. They were saying something like he, the man, would get really mean soon.

She had the impression that what they really meant was something ugly because as they were whispering, a little brown-haired girl of about 8 years with long, thick, curly locks was walking down a path near the house. Jez realized it was she. It was like she was seeing from outside her little self, in her own world, happily walking along, enjoying the noonday sun and the flowers that grew on a hill along her path. She wore a scarf with a blue flower in it. Her dress was loose at various points. She was a radiant and beautiful little image walking along the path as if on her way to some important, happy occasion.

The man was looking out the window in the workshop at the little girl. The little boys were talking about what he might do to them if they stayed around, but they, seeing the little girl, were relieved that his eye had caught on her while he was drinking. They ran off.

Jezereal rubbed her forehead and face, thinking about how little Jez woke up confused and hurting "down there" one night. Sitting there trying to recall the memory, she couldn't fully reconstruct it. In her imagination, she looked to her left, and he was lying beside her. A dirty, once-white, cotton sheet covered him. She lay with nothing, and she felt the chill. She was silent. Then, in her memory, or was it her memory, or why was she seeing that? She felt her momma rolling her away from the man. She feigned sleep.

Petsy quietly picked her up in her arms and carried her off. As she carried her, tears ran from her eyes and dropped on Jezereal. Petsy wiped her tears from the little Jez's face with her lips, and hugged her close while her own body shook from holding back more tears. Sitting there face full in the window, her mind years in the past, she was still confused and horrified.

Jezereal awakened from her nightmare when she heard the call from the porter that those who were to depart at Philadelphia would be helped with their baggage if needed. She roused herself, constantly blinking to clear her eyesight, and she stepped warily off the train and followed him. She was dressed as a man, a soldier, so she doubted he would make anything of her in his vicinity.

She watched the man as he strode toward a tavern. Yes, it was Rory. She followed him in and went around the back of the tavern to the bar. She asked for a room. She would watch him from afar but near enough to be in earshot. She began to frequent the bar each night. She took each man as he came, dined and supped with some, and gambled with others until she felt secure enough of their confidence to be familiar with the particulars of their schemes.

Meanwhile, it had been ascertained that on the Baltimore Railroad line, there were men engaged in military drilling. Several other detectives were employed by the chief to discover those organizations' purpose; disguised as laborers or farm hands, they got themselves mustered in. One of the military companies proved to be loyal; another, under the pretense of being prepared to guard one or more of the bridges north of Baltimore, was designed for quite the opposite purpose. Having this intelligence was the reason she had been contacted in the first place. Something was potentially afoot that wasn't particularly military-focused, yet politically focused, ridding the government of its leader.

One night, when all who were regulars got to whispering and drinking, Jez heard something that she had to lean in to hear. The men were almost giggling about how they could steal Lincoln off the train on his way home over the bridge. She dropped her head and stared into her drink. Rory was in on it with them and was going to play a part in the conspiracy to kill the President. Listening, she realized ten years had not changed him. Seeing his own boys die due to drinking didn't disturb him. One got himself stabbed to death in a drunken brawl, and the other simply drank so much one night that he didn't wake up the next day. Young men both, but even that was not enough for him to wonder what he had done to make them that way. But, as it was most likely, he didn't have enough affection for them to feel anything other than they had always been worthless burdens anyway.

In truth, if that was the case, she had not felt much for either of them. To her, miscreants were all they could have been with a daddy like that, with no mother or anybody else to soften or protect them. As it was, Jezereal surmised that they were spawned from that source that threatened to populate the earth with more of them than humans. She remembered how they looked like animals to her as a child. She remembered many a day walking home, trying to ignore them, but that had never worked.

They cursed her, yanked at her hair, punched her in her breast, and stabbed her with sticks in her genital area. She tried to ignore them. What else could she do without bringing worse down upon her? Then she tried to be nice to them. She had stolen slices of cake and cookies and bought them with her several times, hoping they would stop being mean to her, but that didn't work either. They'd simply eat her cake and cookies and then taunt and terrorize her. She'd learned from them that hurt people hurt other people, but at the time, she didn't know how deeply they'd been hurt.

From the moment she had seen Rory, she knew the night would come, and they would both meet their destiny. It would reveal either a further trek upon the road of life on earth or their removal from the journey. So, even before she left the market, she began to pray. She knew it would be their night of reckoning; she would make it so. She was tired of his spirit invading hers, and she would be loosed from it. She observed from a distance him entering Pickler's Tavern. From that point in time, she knew she had another three hours wait. He was a creature of habit, and she knew that his bravado, money, tavern keeps, and patrons' endurance would only last that long.

After she witnessed his entrance, she located herself down the road he had to travel on his way home. As she sat waiting, she stretched out upon the back of the buckboard, running scriptures through her mind of people who had changed, who had been enlightened by the Word; she prayed for this man. Intermittent between the passages, she heard Kaylean's words, ominous and contradictory to her resolve, "Jezzie, never test a man beyond what you believe he can pass." Right or wrong, she prayed that ten years' time and the death of his boys was enough for him to change. Maybe he could pass the test. And, if he could pass the test, maybe she could forgive. Maybe she could find the right in the world.

So, about an hour later, she entered the tavern as a woman. She feigned a woman in distress. She'd asked where another livery was located as she needed a carriage. She had just wanted him to help her or leave her alone, let her make her way home. Why couldn't he, at least this time, just help someone or leave the person alone? That would not be him. She sat and waited for the barkeep to slow down in order to ask the question. In the meantime, Rory had approached her and asked if he could help her find her way. She thanked him but said, "No, I can find it with a bit of information from the owner here." He told her, "You see, he's busy. Come on girl, I'll help you find it." She knew the swaying of his body and the glint in his eye. Jezereal snapped way back to the little girl sitting in Momma Kaylean's backyard. Cracked her neck and said, "Sir, that is so kind of you. Yes, please show me the way."

When she returned to herself, only then, looking down upon the sorry piece of shit that lay cowering and screaming before her did she think maybe he didn't know how much he had hurt her beyond just her physical body? Maybe somebody had hurt him the same way. And she lost the will to kill him. Unfortunately for him, he saw the softening look of compassion in her eye...the lack of will to kill. He stopped crying and begging for his life. His eyes that had a moment before been wide in recognition of who she was and, in terror, narrowed, and then he hissed with spittle dripping from his lips. "You dirty suckling of a whore, I'll kill you, like I killed that dog bitch mother of your'n."

Jezereal stepped back and marveled upon this man. At that exact moment, Jez did not even feel the stirring of revenge she thought she would feel. There was once a time when she wanted to wreck upon him because he killed her mother. In fact, Jezereal almost had the urge to laugh at how his lips screwed to the side in deep rage. He was a cornered animal, and this was the best he could do to assert himself.

Even with his hands tied and roped to knees, ass in the air with his genitals displayed, he could somehow feel as if he still had the upper hand, that she was the weak one? There was just no backing down in him, no ability to think his way through his situation. She cocked her head and stretched her neck until it touched her right shoulder. It was stiff and sore, but from experience, she knew how to relieve the stiffness: Vigorous activity. She had to check herself and disregard the impact on her own emotions. The hatred in Rory's eye reminded her that there was nothing funny about this; he would kill her if he could.

"Enough! She said firmly to him as she cracked her neck and steadied her gaze upon him. She took note that fear had returned to his eyes wordlessly and soundlessly as she moved to the fireplace. She stood for a second, stooped down, and then turned back toward him with a burning log in her hand. She blew out the flame upon it. She raised the log over her head with her eyes to the ceiling and whispered something un-intelligible to him. He cursed her...one last time...as she brought the smoldering log down into his mouth. His flesh sizzled and turned black. She held it there. She held it while she whispered to him, "No more foulness shall come from thy lips or from thy loins ever again."

She held it as he struggled against the stick and her weight upon it. When he stopped struggling and clawing at the air be-tween them, she relaxed her weight. When there was no more struggle, she sat back on the bed. No prayer in her arsenal had preserved him from this moment. She examined him and the stick that protruded from his mouth. She absently yanked at it, tearing flesh with it, and then she whacked him across the fore-head with it. She felt the urge to hit him there again but realized it would do no good. He was dead or so near to it, and his last verbal display showed that he would not ever understand that he could not, if he lived should not, hurt her or anyone else and get away with it.

So, she sat on the bed beside him until the impulse subsided, until her anger at him began to drain away, and she felt noth-ing for him or what he had done to her mother or to her. She sat until she knew he would never haunt her dreams or life ever again.

Jezereal stepped outside without stopping to pull on any clothing. Her step went from resolved and firm to unsteady. By the time she reached the front step, her whole body was shaking violently. She was dizzy, and although the cool evening breeze helped to bring down the heat that pumped from her body, it wasn't enough to stop her stomach from heaving. She tried to stop it, but the acid began to burn the back of her throat, and the taste of bile surging couldn't be stopped, and she vomited in wave after wave. She heaved until there was nothing left, yet she continued to wretch. She felt as if there was gravel in her throat, and it was tearing at her esophagus. But she kept going until she pissed herself. She couldn't hold it because her spasms were too intense.

Finally able to stand up, pull her shoulders back, and wipe the sweat from her forehead, she considered, "I can't trust anyone around here. Potential conspirators may be anybody. They may be like me, acting like someone they are not. They can be any-where, and time is growing short until those who are plotting a plan to carry out the deed. What am I going to do?" The only thing she could think to do was to go prevail on Gil for help. He would most likely turn her down; she knew he would. She just couldn't let him, though. This was too important.

~~~~

She had journeyed in search of Gil and found him. Two battle-worn horses trudged slowly along the muddy path, drag-ging her carriage, whose left front wheel squeaked desperately upon each complete revolution. The full moon of that evening intermittently illuminated between stands of trees the contents of their lot: Jezereal, nodding against sleep and absently en-couraging them forward with the reigns, a precious cargo, and a broken man passed out from drink and a solid blow to his left temple. The groves of trees lining their way stood tall and firm in the drunken soil. Jezzie tried to draw strength from their defiance of the wind and rain from the night before.
~~~~

She was so weary and ready to sleep that she might have enjoyed even a conversation with Gil, who was still slumped forward in the seat beside her. She had knocked him out cold. She wondered for a brief moment if she'd hit him too hard, perhaps given him a concussion. "Oh, well," she thought, resisting the temptation to worry. Hopefully, she hadn't damaged him too much. But, at the time, it was the only thing she could think of to get him to come along. Perhaps she could have sweet-talked him into the journey if she'd had more time, but she doubted it. Her sweet-talkin' days were long gone.

"Gil, I need you on this," she had said the night before. He had laughed at her. "Now, Jezzie, you don't need anyone or anything. Why you comin' here tonight to say you need me on somethin'? Whatever it is, if you can't take care of it yourself, it doesn't need to be taken care of." But, she knew that was his way of trying to flatter his way out of work. All he wanted to do at this point in his life was to drink, sleep, relieve himself, and start all over again. He was no longer driven by nature to get between a woman's thighs, and he definitely considered his fighting days to be over. Both had taken their toll on his body, his mind and he thought his soul. No need to ever fight again for anything was his belief. So, she figured if she just knocked him in the head, then he wouldn't have to make the decision to at least get on the road; she'd have made it for him.

Some people just don't know when they still have something else to give, and they have to be shown that they do. So, she did what she had to do. When he turned his back to reach behind him for another bottle, she had picked up the one they'd both drained and hit him square in the side of the head with it. He barely flinched after the hit. He turned back to her in his chair, looked straight at her, and said, "Jezzie, you're one sound bitch. You done knocked me out." She raised an eyebrow, wondering how that could possibly be true with him still talking to her, and at that, his eyes closed, and he fell forward face down on the table.

She stood and rounded the table to his side, pulled his head up by the back of his hair, and said, "Gilly, honey, I'm sorry. I can't explain why I need you, but for some reason, I do. I'm scared honey, and if you're with me, I can meet this task, I think. So, come on you." She'd have never called him honey to his face if he were conscious. It would have been unnatural on her lips and on his ears. She pulled his torso sideways and slipped her arms under his, and leveraging her weight and his against the floor, she pulled him from his seat. She managed through sheer will to get him outside the front door. He wasn't quite as tall as Lincoln, but perhaps they could divert the persons on the train, and Lincoln could escape another way.

For a man who loved being in the mix of things at times, even unconscious, he bore his spirit well. She was sweating profusely with the effort, and once outside the cool wind and rain both chilled her and quickened her thinking. How on earth was she going to get him into the wagon? She dropped his arms onto the porch and used her boot as a ramp to let his head slide to the porch floor. She stepped over him and pulled her shawl close around her neck and face as she stepped off the porch. If she could have, she'd have chosen a better evening to kidnap her brother, but this night she didn't have the luxury of choosing or letting him decide. He was coming with her, and that was that. She hoped that when he awakened on the road, he wouldn't be too mad or stubborn to want to turn back. Hopefully, his hangover and the pain in his head would quiet any dissension. But, no matter. She had enough whiskey on the buckboard to get him through when she needed him.

~ Twelve ~

SPIRITING LINCOLN FROM THE TRAPS OF THE CONSPIRATORS

Jez had telegraphed what she'd heard the men whispering. They planned to take Lincoln when he was on the train from Philadelphia to Maryland. She proposed in her mind a distraction, which would be Gil. If he "packaged" him right, someone might guess it's Lincoln in costume. Gil woke up the next morning in a hotel room and had no idea of where he was. Soon after his awakening, Jez stood near his bed.

"Aw, shit, no. What do you think you're doing!?"

"Gil..."

"No, no, don't Gil me! Where are we, and why you got me here?"

Jezereal folded her hands together and looked out of the side of her and then down and said, "I need your help."

"No, no, not this time. I don't care what it is. I'll not be a part of whatever it is you got going on in your head or your government or anything. Excuse me, I'm just gonna get up and get back home and do what I was doing before you assaulted me. Won't fall for that again."

"You won't even listen to me? It's vital."

"Nope, I don't want to hear any of it. I told you I'm through. Why can't you leave me alone? Go find your other man or another man. I'm in the wings...no, I'm not in the play at all." Jezereal sat quietly. Maybe he was going to leave her there alone. She sat and thought while he dressed and decided that there wasn't much she could do. The other agents were going to move the president on another train at night, and maybe that's all that would be needed. Not much she could do except for one thing.

She excused herself and said she wanted to run to the store and that she'd be back in time for them to have supper before they left. Gil crawled back into bed. She went shopping. She got back, and he was up and ready to eat. They went to a local inn to eat a sumptuous dinner. They had a few drinks. Well, he had a few more than her. They boarded the train; however, he didn't notice it was bound for Maryland. It was still misty out, and she had cloaked him well and helped him to a seat in the back of the train's passenger seating.

As he drifted into deep sleep, she placed a six-pipe hat on his that she'd bought in town and sat across from him with her gun under her shawl. It happened as she thought it would. The conspirators stopped the train, and they raced to the back, where she and Gil sat and pulled their guns. Turmoil broke out in the train. Gil woke up and shouted, "What in the hell is this?"

The men looked stunned. It was not Mr. Lincoln. They turned and rushed off the train. As the tumult died down and Gil looked to his feet, he saw the hat on the floor. He looked to Jezereal and pursed his lips, preventing himself from spewing what was in his head. He had been played. He shook his head in full knowledge. When they arrived in Maryland, there was no explaining to be done. Jez reported the thwarted attack to the White House once they arrived. Gil refused to leave the station, got a return ticket, and shooed her away from him as she lingered at the station.

Jezereal didn't sit near him but watched him while he sat. As he rose to stand in line for the train, she went near him. Gil turned to her and said, "Let this be the last time I ever have to look at you," and boarded the train to return home.

She was happy that the greater picture had unfolded well. No one was hurt. However, she was devastated that the relationship was perhaps burnt. She reported the escapade and was told that the president thanked her for her work on his behalf. He wished that no one knew about the potential attack or any others he had undergone since his election.

It wasn't necessary to seed any more unrest in the people. Jez went back to the train station the next day and took the train home to Gil. It would take a while for him to forgive her. This she knew, but where else was there to go?

Lincoln's Second Inaugural Address

Shortly after that, in April, the war was over. General Lee surrendered at Appomattox in Virginia. Jezereal was living in the country not too far from Gil. She was resting on the porch when she received the news.

"All praise" she gave to God. She was tired and fell into a sound sleep. Several days later, she read the newspaper that recounted Lincoln's inaugural address:

"Fellow countrymen: At this second appearing to take the oath of the presidential office, there is less occasion for an extended address than there was at the first. Then, a statement, somewhat in detail, of a course to be pursued, seemed fitting and proper. Now, at the expiration of four years during which public declarations have been constantly called forth on every point and phase of the great contest which still absorbs the attention and engrosses the energies of the nation little that is new could be presented.

The progress of our arms, upon which all else chiefly depends is as well known to the public as to myself and it is I trust reasonably satisfactory and encouraging to all. With high hope for the future no prediction in regard to it is ventured.

On the occasion corresponding to this four years ago all thoughts were anxiously directed to an impending civil war. All dreaded it ～ all sought to avert it. While the inaugural address was being delivered from this place devoted altogether to saving the Union without war insurgent agents were in the city seeking to destroy it without war ～ seeking to dissolve the Union and divide effects by negotiation.

Both parties deprecated war but one of them would make war rather than let the nation survive, and the other would accept war rather than let it perish. And the war came. One eighth of the whole population was colored slaves, not distributed generally over the union but localized in the southern part of it. These slaves constituted a peculiar and powerful interest.

All knew that this interest was somehow the cause of the war. To strengthen perpetuate and extend this interest was the object for which the insurgents would rend the Union even by war while the government claimed no right to do more than to restrict the territorial enlargement of it.

Neither party expected for the war the magnitude or the duration which it has already attained. Neither anticipated that the cause of the conflict might cease with or even before the conflict itself should cease. Each looked for an easier triumph and a result less fundamental and astounding.

Both read the same Bible and pray to the same God and each invokes His aid against the other. It may seem strange that any men should dare to ask a just God's assistance in wringing their bread from the sweat of other men's faces but let us judge not that we be not judged. The prayers of both could not be answered ~ that of neither has been answered fully. The Almighty has His own purposes.

"Woe unto the world because of offenses for it must needs be that offenses come but woe to that man by whom the offense cometh." If we shall suppose that American slavery is one of those offenses which in the providence of

God must needs come but which having continued through His appointed time He now wills
to remove and that He gives to both North
and South this terrible war as the woe due to
those by whom the offense came shall we discern therein any departure from those divine
attributes which the believers in a living God
always ascribe to Him. Fondly do we hope ~ fervently do we pray ~ that this mighty scourge of
war may speedily pass away.

Yet, if God wills that it continue until all the
wealth piled by the bondsman's two hundred
and fifty years of unrequited toil shall be sunk
and until every drop of blood drawn with the
lash shall be paid by another drawn with the
sword as was said three thousand years ago so
still it must be said 'the judgments of the Lord
are true and righteous altogether.

With malice toward none with charity for all
with firmness in the right as God gives us to see
the right let us strive on to finish the work, we
are in to bind up the nation's wounds, to care
for him who shall have borne the battle and for
his widow and his orphan ~ to do all which may
achieve and cherish a just and lasting peace
among ourselves and with all nations."

She sat in silence after reading it, rocking her body. "It is
over; it's finally over. Life can only get better for all of us now."

Lincoln's Assassination

It was Good Friday. Their reunion had been and still was uneasy, but over the days of just being near her, they settled into a quiet peace. Gil was coming in from catching fish for dinner. Jezereal was outside hanging clothing on the line to dry when a rider rode swiftly by shouting, "Lincoln is dead! Lincoln is dead!" She stood stunned for a minute. Initially, Jezereal thought it was an April joke and took no heed of it except that it continued to grow throughout the town. A young telegraph delivery boy knocked on her door. She thanked him and tipped him while wondering what she was receiving. It was a notice from Carver dated the 16th. The rumors on the street were true. He stated that President Lincoln was shot by John Wilkes Booth in the Ford Theater on Good Friday, April 14, and died the next day. Her body shuttered and started shaking. Jezereal knew about Booth because she had seen him in plays. He and his family were re-nowned actors whose paths had crossed Vestvali's through various theaters throughout the country and abroad. Standing there alone in the house. She crumpled onto a settee. She couldn't even cry. All she could think was, "All of this for nothing?"

She went to bed and didn't get back out for several days. She woke up one morning to the sound of her own snoring. She tried to shake herself awake out of the darkness in her soul and the misery. She had the sense she had fallen into an abyss, and the sound was like sunlight beaconing her. In her mind, she listened to the sound and then sensed light. She looked up toward the faint light. She had been trying to climb out of the black, wet, jagged rocks to get a foothold here and there, sometimes slipping and falling backward. She kept trying to get a handle.

It was that morning that she got near the top and heard Gil calling her name. She saw him looking down upon her. She called to him, and he reached into the cavern and pulled her up. As she came to, she asked, "Where am I?"

Jezereal on Hill

She could see the long trail of black smoke in the distance. The train was coming that carried Lincoln. Her tears ran freely down her face. There are times when you cry when staunching the flow is sacrilegious. Some things need to be cried over. She prayed for this man's soul. Then, she prayed for the soul of the nation.

Carver stood just inside the door of the front walkway at his post near the back of the caboose. He had seen people at every stop along the way dressed in black or whatever clothing they had, mourning their lost leader. Now, in the outland between cities and towns, where there was nothing but green land and clear blue sky, he wept within himself. What would this land become now? He had hanged his every hope for a rational, compassionate, and free United States on Lincoln, but now, with Lincoln gone, his dream was gone as well.

He glimpsed an image out of place amongst the greenness of the trees and blueness of the skies in a grove coming closer up over and around the bend of the tracks. His senses were immediately alerted, and he strained to scan the oddity. It appeared to be a woman resting her hand on a cane. As he drew closer, he drew his rifle to the ready as he realized that the lone figure stood not with a cane or a stick. It was a woman standing tall and proud in a black dress and bonnet. At her side stood ready a rifle, which, as the train passed by, she shouldered and aimed high into the air.

She pulled the trigger and saluted the president's train as it passed. Carver could have pulled the trigger on his rifle, but as her aim was high, he conceded no danger to the train itself and its passengers and stood down his rifle. Carver couldn't be sure, but his heart skipped a beat, which told him that he knew this woman. By her stature and manner, it could be none other than Jezereal. The magnificence of the man who lay in state under his guard and the equal magnificence of the lone figure of the woman standing on the hillside with her rifle nearly brought him to tears, but he held it in. Hope was not lost. Perhaps, in some way, it had only just begun.

About the Author

C. Jenkins was born in the North and raised in the Midwest, with family primarily from the Southeast, a member of the Cherokee Nation in Tahlequah, Oklahoma. She currently lives in the southeast part of Nebraska.

She is a licensed mental health practitioner (LMHP), a licensed massage therapist (LMT), and holds a PhD in Social Psychology. She's a mother of one son with three grandsons.

She enjoys walks in nature and reading old books of various genres, fiction and nonfiction alike. She loves reading the personal diaries of others and rereading her own, which leads her to contemplate our collective conscious/unconscious perceptions and inspirations of the past and present and what they portend for the future.

C. Jenkins began writing due to her insightful thoughts about life as it resonated with her inner being. *Jezereal A Woman's Life Memoirs* is book one of the many and only the beginning of her journey as an author.

www.ingramcontent.com/pod-product-compliance
Lightning Source LLC
Chambersburg PA
CBHW031539310726
48971CB00008B/2552